Books by Samantha Winston

Single Titles

Time Tracker

Time Tracker

ISBN # 978-1-78686-134-4

©Copyright Samantha Winston 2017

Cover Art by Posh Gosh ©Copyright 2017

Interior text design by Claire Siemaszkiewicz

Totally Bound Publishing

TIME TRACKER

SAMANTHA WINSTON

Chapter One

Allie O'Shea closed the heavy, leather-bound book she'd been reading at her desk and looked at the man standing in her doorway. He wore a crisp gray suit, a navy tie and a CIA pin on his lapel. His presence wasn't a surprise because he'd made an appointment to see her, but it was a mystery. He hadn't said what his visit was about, only that it was urgent and strictly private.

Allie motioned for him to sit in the chrome seat in front of her glass-topped desk and she leaned forward in her chair. "What can I do for you, Mr. Smith?"

"My presence here is top secret," he said. "Before I say anything more, you'll have to sign this nondisclosure contract." He set a sheaf of paper on her desk. "Just read the last line and sign here, please."

She started to grin. This must be a joke. Who would pull such a stunt on her, though? The grin slid off her face. Nobody would, not in this building. No one teased her anymore. This wasn't first grade where her short, stocky stature had earned her the nickname Minnie. She worked with serious, highly trained, dedicated people who rarely smiled much less cracked jokes. In the short time she'd worked at the Farmington Institute of Dead Languages, no one had ever displayed the slightest interest in her except professionally. So this must be real. But what could the CIA want with her? She decided to say yes to his demand. If the CIA wanted to play secret spy games, she would go along.

She pulled the papers to her, read them and signed on the dotted line. It all appeared legit. "All right, I swear. What is this about?"

"Do you remember reading about the man found in the Arctic Circle last year?"

"An Iron Age man in perfectly preserved condition found in the tundra beneath the permafrost." She paused, and a spark of interest pricked her. "Did you find some writing in his belongings? Is that it?"

"Before I say anything else, I want you to sign another paper. It states you will never divulge anything about the mission involved." He handed her a single paper.

Odd, she'd already signed his nondisclosure statement. What was this? Allie examined the document. It stipulated she could never speak about the mission to anyone, no reports were to be written, no photographs taken, nothing, or else she would be liable for damages. What damages? In short, it said that if she blabbed, she would regret it for the rest of her life — financially she would be ruined, and legally she could be put in jail. She frowned. It was extreme for a legal document. She had never seen another contract like this one. Usually they were only valid until the final report was published, but this one specified until the end of her life.

"Hardly the best way to start a working relationship," she said, frowning at the legalese.

"It is to protect us, but it will also protect you. Anything that happens to you as a result of this project will be entirely our responsibility. And you will be handsomely rewarded."

Okay, she was hooked. She took her pen and signed her name with a flourish. "There. Is that all? Can you tell me about the writings you found?"

Mr. Smith put his hands on her desk and leaned forward. "It's not exactly that, Ms. O'Shea. We need you because..." He paused and for the first time seemed uncertain.

She saw his hesitation and thought she knew why. "I'm older than I look. My specialty is ancient languages including cuneiform and Celtic. If you found something written in his belongings, I think I can help you. I can't be certain unless I see it, though."

"Ms. O'Shea, we know all about you. What we need is a translator. You see, the man in question is being reanimated in a station in Alaska. We have kept this absolutely confidential because of the repercussions of such an act. Surely you can understand the need for secrecy in this situation."

Allie suddenly had trouble breathing. "Wait a minute. Hold on. Did you say reanimated? Are you saying that he's...? That he's...?"

"Alive. Yes. Let me explain. It seems our Iron Age man's body was in suspended animation, flash-frozen, as it were, and when we started thawing him out, one of the scientists had the crazy idea of running an electrical current through his body." He gave a shrug. "Why refuse? The guy had been dead for thousands of years. Nobody could have predicted what happened next."

"His heart started beating." Allie swallowed hard. "How long has he been in reanimation? He's got to be brain-dead, though, right?"

The man shook his head. "All I know is that as soon as they saw the heartbeat, they stopped everything. The brain had to be protected at all costs. If anything went wrong, all they'd have would be a two-thousand-year-old vegetable. Our man has been in reanimation for nine months. His brainwaves seem perfectly normal. We're ready to wake him up now, and we want to be able to speak to him. We need someone who speaks his language. Otherwise, he'll be completely disoriented."

Allie grimaced. He would be completely disoriented no matter what.

As if reading her mind, Mr. Smith continued, "He's in a special environment, made to resemble as much as possible as an Iron Age dwelling. You'll be there when he wakes up."

"When exactly will that be?" Disbelief warred with amazement and excitement. An Iron Age man! What incredible things he could teach them!

"In three days. I'm sorry to be so abrupt, but you have to leave tomorrow. Your superiors know that you are needed on a sensitive case. We have contacted them already. But you will give no details. Please read all the papers in the contract that I'll leave with you and bring them to the airport tomorrow. Meet me at terminal four, Air Alaska. Seven a.m. Don't bring much. You won't be staying more than a week so they'll never even miss you here." He handed her a heavy manila envelope, upon which lay a plane ticket. First class for Alaska.

Her mouth went dry. "If you did any research on me at all, you know I don't fly. I can get there by train, can't I?"

The man's eyes grew icy. "No, Ms. O'Shea. There is a very tight time schedule. This is of the highest importance. Any refusal to cooperate fully will result in your immediate exclusion from this program. I assume you wish to work on this project? You'll be well paid. We've taken the liberty of tripling your normal fee."

She did wish to work on the project, and the money didn't matter. She had to go. She had to see this man, talk to him and communicate with someone from the past. This was an amazing opportunity and she wouldn't pass it up, even if she was sure to perish in a terrible plane wreck. She would think about that later. She nodded curtly. "I'll be there."

Mr. Smith left without shaking her hand. Allie took the papers out of the envelope and carefully read at the contract. Sign on the dotted line. If they had asked her to sign in blood, she would have. An opportunity like this happened maybe once in a lifetime.

The contract seemed in order. It was for a translator in ancient languages for the duration of one week. Her job would consist of translating the words of a man who had been in suspended animation for twenty centuries. She would assist the scientists when he woke up. After one week, she would be free to leave. A small part of her brain wondered why the contract was for such a short time. Normally a study like this would last for years. Maybe it was just a test, to see how she did. If she was able to speak to him, they might keep her on for longer. Hopefully they would let her write a paper on her findings. She would publish it and be famous. The woman who spoke to the past — she could just see the headlines.

She picked up her phone and buzzed the institute's secretary. "This is Allie O'Shea, I'm going on a short trip. I'll be gone no more than seven days. Call Dr. Jarvis and let her know I'll be late with the translation, but I'll get it to her as soon as possible." Now all she had to do was pack and get the strongest sedative on the market for the plane trip.

* * * *

The trip had been easier than she had dared dream. The pills had worked their magic and she had slept through the entire flight, only waking up when the plane had landed. Thanks to the miracles of modern medicine she could fly!

The grogginess left by the pills wore off as she got her luggage and followed Mr. Smith through the busy air terminal. *Wait a minute. The exit is that way.* She tapped his arm. "Excuse me. Why are we going toward gates one through ten?"

"We're taking a private plane to the Air Force base. You didn't think our station would be located in the middle of a city, did you? We're going to a secret military station in the Arctic."

Did he just say take a plane? Panic froze her limbs and she stumbled. Oh, God. If she died of a heart attack, would they be able to revive her at that secret station?

The airplane looked too small to fly. It perched on the icy tarmac like a child's toy. Allie's teeth chattered and her hands felt like blocks of ice.

She could hardly fasten her seatbelt. When the plane took off she jumbled all her prayers together and squeezed her eyes shut. Then the plane hit a cloud, started to bounce, and she nearly passed out.

* * * *

"Miss O'Shea, you can open your eyes now. We've arrived." Mr. Smith sounded exasperated.

Tough. She opened one eye, then another. "It's night." She unclenched her fingers from the arm of the seat and she glanced at her watch. They had only been in the air for two hours. Two hours of holding on as tightly as she could, gritting her teeth, and gasping every time the plane had hit turbulence. It shouldn't be dark yet.

"We're above the Arctic Circle. It's dark most of the time. Get up and get your things. I hope you brought a warmer coat than that," he added, glancing at her down jacket.

Above the Arctic Circle? *Where is this secret base?* "I'm impervious to cold," she said, shrugging into her plum-colored jacket and making sure she had her purse and luggage. She stepped out of the plane and a gust of frigid wind knocked her sideways. She skidded on ice and would have fallen, but a soldier dressed in a white snowsuit grabbed her and pushed her toward a door, seemingly set into a snow bank.

Before entering, she turned and looked back at the airfield. She saw nothing but ice and snow. No buildings anywhere, only a line of blue lights showing the runway. The plane engines roared as it turned and trundled back down the runway and took off, vanishing into the immense arctic night. Then the blue runway lights were extinguished. Nothing was left but murky darkness and whispering snow. A shiver tightened her belly and she entered the station.

Warmth and light greeted her at the end of a narrow tunnel. She stopped and stared. As huge as an airplane hangar, the underground station was like a set from a sci-fi movie. She stood at the top of a metal platform and watched a beehive of activity.

Harsh neon lights dazzled her eyes. A steady electrical hum formed a background to the sound of echoing footsteps, the murmur of voices and the rustle of papers.

Everyone, it seemed, carried a clipboard.

Hesitantly, she walked toward a pod elevator where Mr. Smith motioned impatiently.

"You can sightsee later. I have to introduce you to the group leader, Captain Bide. The man is waking up faster than we expected. Hurry!"

His words jolted her out of her stupor and she rushed to the pod. Her luggage didn't fit, so she left it on the platform.

"Leave it there, someone will bring it to your room," Mr. Smith informed her tersely.

The pod slid down a cable like a ski lift and deposited them next to a low building in the middle of the hangar. A crowd stood at the doorway, and as she got out of the pod, a tall, thin man in a white lab coat ran to her and grabbed her hand.

"No time for chit-chat. Let's get you dressed now. The subject is nearly awake and we can't wait any longer."

The next few minutes flew by in a blur while she took off all her clothes in a cubicle and pulled on a leather dress, leather boots and a bear-claw necklace. *A bear-claw necklace?* She made a face as she touched one of the long, sharp claws.

"That will impress him. You'll be a shaman, all right?" A gray-haired woman with a clipboard poked her head in the cubicle and beamed at her. "Let's hurry now. No time to talk. Come on!"

Before she could protest that the necklace was a bad idea, Allie found her arm in the grip of a muscular man who jogged her to a small door set in the wall.

"Don't be alarmed. He seems groggy but he's rapidly gaining consciousness. We'll be following everything with a camera and we'll be able to hear everything you say."

"What exactly is my mission?" she asked, dashing along at his side.

"Just find out who he is and where he came from. Good luck." He opened the door and shoved her inside.

She found herself in what she imagined was a Viking longhouse. A nude man lay on a furry pallet near the fire.

Firelight ran over his body, gilding it and showing flowing muscles beneath his smooth skin. He had dark brown hair, cut short and lifting in curls off his temples. Not very tall, but exceedingly well made and strong, the man's physique took her breath away. Her nipples tingled and her belly tightened in a purely animalistic response at the sight of his nudity. He moaned and stirred, but his eyes remained closed.

With her heart somewhere in her throat, she crept toward him, stopping long enough to take off the stupid bear-claw necklace. If he were a Celt or a Norseman, the necklace would frighten and confuse him. A young woman would not wear such a symbol of power — only a very old woman could aspire to such trappings.

She kneeled by the pallet and shook her head. He would not like waking up on the floor either. He should be on a bed. There were some beds set in deep wall niches, with thick, soft furs and embroidered hangings. He should be in one of those.

She peered upward, trying to spot the camera. They hadn't tried to hide it, probably figuring the man wouldn't be looking for it. A small camera peered out of a chink in the wall. She waved at it and asked, "Can someone come inside and help me get him into a decent bed?"

The door opened. A man poked in his head and whispered agitatedly, "Do not, I repeat, do not try to contact us. Pretend you are in a primitive land and just do what you have to do. We will not come in unless your life is in danger. And Dr. Paula says to put the necklace back on." He glared at her and shut the door.

She sighed and looked down at the man.

Dark brown eyes stared back at her. He wore a puzzled expression, but didn't act as though he were frightened. He studied her for a long moment, his eyes going from her hair to her feet. Then they settled on her breasts. His eyebrows lifted a fraction.

Hot blood burned her cheeks, then she remembered. She

had forgotten to take off the silver crescent moon necklace she always wore. It lay between her breasts, probably a glaring anachronism that would send the man into hysterics.

He cleared his throat and a few guttural sounds came out. Nothing she recognized as speech. *Great, I won't be of any help at all.*

Then he lifted himself onto one elbow. "I have great thirst."

His voice was halting and ragged, but she understood. Granted, the accent didn't sound like anything she had ever heard, but she'd understood what he had meant. He spoke Latin, but hesitantly, in a strange dialect. Who was he and where had he come from? So many questions jumbled in her head.

He coughed and pointed to his throat. "Do you have anything to drink?"

"A thousand pardons," she said. A pitcher of water stood nearby and she poured him a cup. Everything was made of glazed pottery. She wondered if it seemed odd to him.

He sat up and drank, the water moving in knots down his throat. He wiped his arm across his mouth and nodded. "Thank ye."

"You speak Latin. Are you Roman?" She'd read that he had been found in northern Scandinavia. *Could he be a Roman soldier?*

He rubbed his hands over his face. "Nay. I am Celt from the kingdom of Celtica."

"You speak Latin well." She couldn't take her eyes off him. Never had she seen such a handsome man. He seemed as unaware of his nudity as a wild animal. Then he stretched and flexed his muscles, testing his arms and legs as he spoke.

"I also speak Greek, Pictish, Phoenician and Iberian —" He broke off and gazed at her thoughtfully. "I know not who you are, nor where I am. 'Tis strange. I can recall the tongues of man, but not my own name." He gestured toward the room. "This place calls not to my memory.

Where am I?"

Perhaps he would be more comfortable speaking his own language, though his Latin was passable. In Celtic, she said, "You have been ill for a long time. We brought you here to heal your wounds. My name is Allie."

His eyes widened. "You speak Celtic?"

She hadn't considered what to tell him about herself. "My father was Celt." Well, close enough. He was Irish. "Can you remember your name?"

He closed his eyes then opened them. "I seem to hear the name Kell, but whether it is mine or not, I cannot be sure."

"I'll call you Kell then. Perhaps it will help you remember."

"You wear the pendant of the crescent moon. Are you an adept of the moon goddess?" His fingertip nearly touched her skin, stopping a hair's breadth from the pendant.

She could sense the heat emanating from his body, and a shiver ran through her. "No. This belonged to my mother."

"Ah." The man drew back slightly and examined his surroundings, his eyes taking in every detail. "You said we brought me to this place. Where are the others?"

"They have gone...er...hunting." That sounded right. She smiled. "Can you remember your name now?"

He shook his head, his eyes still scanning the room. "In my bones, I feel a strangeness. Is this the land of the dead? I have died, haven't I? And you are the goddess come to carry me to paradise." He chuckled, and before she could react, reached out and touched her breast. "Such a beauty you are. My life on Earth must have been exemplary if the gods sent you to me."

The touch of his hand on her breast sent a delicious tingle through her body, but Allie drew back, her heart pounding. "You are mistaken. You are very much alive. Here, let me get you something to eat."

"I feel no hunger." He shook his head as if to clear it and rubbed a hand over his face. His hand lingered, and he frowned. "Who shaved me?"

"Uh, the healer." Allie gulped. Had he worn a beard

14

when he'd fallen into the icy water? Would he go crazy on her now and attack her, ripping her from limb to limb? She peered at him. No, he appeared perfectly civilized, despite the aura of raw energy that surrounded him.

"A healer?" He cocked an eyebrow at her, and she saw a spark of humor in the depths of his dark-brown eyes. "Are you a healer too? Is that why you watch over me like a mother hawk with her young?"

Had she been staring at him? She lowered her eyes. Would he take offense if she stared at him? She had no idea. "Excuse me. I'm just a foolish woman."

"Why do you beg my pardon?" He reached out and cupped her chin, lifting it so that her eyes met his again. "Don't tell me you're a Greek. The women there are downtrodden, but in my land they are equals."

His gentle touch reassured her. Whatever apprehension she'd had about him vanished. He was no savage.

"No, I'm not Greek."

"I didn't think so. Your speech is strange, but definitely not Greek. I have traveled far, but I've yet to hear someone with your accent." He let go of her chin and sat back, examining her from head to toe. "There is something very strange going on. I cannot recall my own name, and I have no idea where I am or who you are, but I can remember certain things, like the sight of white swans on a small pond and the smell of fresh lavender. Can you tell me who and where I am?" For the first time his voice wavered slightly, as if from fear.

"Do you trust me?" she asked.

He hesitated a long time before he spoke. "Yes, for some reason, I do. I think I must be in the land between the living and the dead. My memories have fled, but my body is still intact. Perhaps I have to accomplish some feat before I can go join my ancestors." He stared at her, his gaze smoldering. "You must be the goddess who will lead me to the land of the dead. I am glad it is you, for you delight me, Allie."

Her cheeks burned. "I am not a goddess and you are not

dead, I promise. Let me get you some more to drink. You must be thirsty."

"No." He kneeled and took her wrist, pressing it to his lips. "You please me, Allie, handmaiden to the gods. Come warm my body with your caresses."

She pulled back, but his grip tightened like a steel trap.

"Let go!"

"Are you married?"

The question surprised her. "No."

"Then I will be gentle." He flashed a grin, surprising her. Still kneeling, he pulled her close and, without letting go of her arm, stroked her hair. "I think I will claim you for my own, maiden Allie." He chuckled. "Your heart races like a hare in flight. I feel your desire. Do you deny it? Come, refuse me no longer." He reached down and stroked his cock, which swelled and hardened.

Allie's mouth went dry. A flood of hot wetness dampened her inner thighs, and she realized she hadn't any panties. Underpants as she knew them didn't exist until the twentieth century, and only men wore braccae or loincloths.

She glanced beseechingly at the camera in the wall. *Please, someone come in here quickly.* But she knew no one would unless he started to hurt her, and he wasn't hurting her at all. Perversely, she wanted him to continue stroking her breast. Her mind grew curiously numb even while her body seemed to come almost painfully alive.

"Kell, please let go of me." She managed to get the words past her lips, all the while wondering what it would be like to feel those strong arms wrapped around her... *No! That is enough!* 'Easy Allie' that's what the boys in school had called her. She had sworn to stop saying 'yes' on the first date. As that thought flitted through her mind, she almost laughed.

"Why do you smile?" Kell released her wrist and stood, stretching languorously. "I have let go of you, but I will have you, Allie. Don't doubt it for a minute."

Another blast of heat soaked her pussy and she almost

groaned aloud. No one had ever looked at her with such a smoldering gaze and said those words to her with so much assurance, as if nothing she could do or say would ever stop him from possessing her. She had to close her eyes to catch her breath and calm her pounding heart. When she opened them, Kell still stood in front of her, his head tilted to the side. As she watched, he rubbed his temples, a line of pain appearing between his eyebrows.

"What is it?" Her voice sounded almost back to normal.

"I am trying to remember this place and how I came to be here, but thinking too hard pains me." He gave a slight grin and shrugged. "I must have hit my head, for I would surely remember meeting a beauty like you." Without waiting for her comment, he strode to the far side of the longhouse. He turned to her, unease written on his features. "I would relieve myself, and then I'd like to bathe. My muscles are stiff and my head still aches. Where is the door?"

Allie swallowed. Where the hell was the bathroom in this place? Clearing her throat, she spoke loudly in the direction of the camera. "You'd like to take a bath, is that it?" At once, she saw a crack of light appear under a hanging deer skin and a door opened slightly. Thank goodness, they must have heard her. Why did they have to hide the damn doors?

"Um, over here, Kell," she said.

Allie had no idea what kind of bathroom a longhouse would possess, so her interest sharpened as she opened the door, pushing aside the deer skin. Inside she saw a wooden bucket of water, a fire, some rocks, a bench, a roughly woven cloth, and another bucket, by itself, behind a standing screen. Oh, joy, the loo. She hoped part of her job did not include emptying the potty.

And what are the stones for? She opened her mouth to ask, but Kell stepped into the room and gave a big smile.

"Ah, a sauna bath." Kell didn't seem to be startled by the details, so it must be authentic, and the stones must be used to make the steam.

"I'll leave you alone." She backed away hurriedly.

He lifted his eyebrow at her. "Who will scrub my back?"

"Scrub your own back." She pointed to a long-handled brush then stepped out of the room, closed the door, and glared at the camera. "What else haven't you shown me?" she hissed.

As before, the hidden door opened a crack and a scientist poked his head in. "We didn't have time to give you the grand tour. If he gets hungry, there are honey cakes in a jar by the fire, and some soup heating in the caldron. Try to get him to tell you what he was doing so far north. Did he tell you what tribe he supposedly belonged to?"

Supposedly? "He's Celt." Allie waited for his exclamation of awe or amazement.

"Celt. Yeah, right." He sounded more bored than amazed. With a shrug, he took a notepad from his pocket and scribbled something. A voice murmured behind him and the scientist nodded.

"Dr. Paula wants you to ask him about his religion, his mating ceremonies and his family structure. Oh, and she says to put the necklace back on right this minute." He rolled his eyes and pulled his head back, the door shutting with a click.

"Great. She wants to know about his mating ceremonies." Allie considered going to scrub Kell's back. That would probably get the mating ceremony going, but she figured she had enough trouble already.

Kell poured the hot water over his head and body, using the ladle. He put water on the hot stones too, making steam. Using handfuls of herbs and soft clay, he scrubbed his skin and hair, then rinsed carefully. He shook his head, making water drops fly. It didn't clear his thoughts, however. Everything stayed muzzy. Almost angrily, he tossed the ladle down and rubbed his hands over his face. Every time he tried to remember who he was or where he was, a stabbing pain hit him.

He threw his head back and closed his eyes, breathing

deeply of the steamy air. He tensed his muscles then relaxed, thinking of the fair maiden waiting in the longhouse. He had never seen such luxurious, deep auburn hair, and her fair, clear skin glowed with health. Her curves would put the goddess of love to shame, and her eyes reminded him of clear, sunlit water running over amber pebbles. Long lashes framed her sparkling eyes, and when her wide mouth curled into a smile, dimples appeared in her cheeks — two dimples, a sign of a lusty appetite for life and love.

Love. He frowned and took the towel from the wooden bench, drying himself as he tried to recall if he had ever had a wife...or even a woman. His cock stirred and hardened when he thought of Allie, so obviously it knew what to do, even though he couldn't remember ever lying between a woman's thighs.

His cock twitched again and he reached down to stroke it. He couldn't think of anything right now except taking Allie in his arms and holding her close to his naked skin. He hoped she would be willing. The looks she had given him, the way her fair skin had flushed when he'd touched her breast, and how her breathing had deepened all told him she had been interested in him. Purely by instinct, he could tell she wanted him. Now he had to convince her to listen to her instincts, and maybe the release he sought would help clear his head.

He opened the door and saw Allie sitting near the fire, her chin in her hands. Quietly, using his hunting skills, he slid through the door and padded across the floor, staying out of sight at her back. He paused, a vague memory stirring in his mind. A wide expanse of snow, trees leaning in the wind, and something breaking beneath his feet. There came an impression of falling into nothingness. He tensed, sudden terror icing his blood, and let out an involuntary cry.

Allie turned and gave a bloodcurdling scream.

Startled, he jumped backward, caught his heel on the edge of a pelt and fell. His head hit the floor with a jolt that made him see stars. Instantly Allie kneeled by his side.

"Kell! I'm sorry. I didn't mean to scream. You scared me, that's all. Are you all right? Answer me!" She cradled his head on her lap and bent over him, her breasts brushing against his chest.

All thoughts of falling or panic fled. His cock stiffened and he managed a grin. "I think I've hurt something. Could you rub it for me?"

"Yes, of course. Where?"

He took her hand and put it on his cock. "Here."

She jumped like a rabbit caught in a snare, but he didn't let go of her wrist.

He got to his knees and faced her, keeping her hand firmly on his member. "Please, Allie. Ease my need. My body aches with longing for you." He shifted his head, trying to catch her gaze. Would she agree? She acted torn in two, this woman. A strange combination of timidity and desire seemed to inhabit her. One moment she stared at him with eyes that blazed. The next, she pulled away.

"Are you a virgin?"

She seemed too old to be one, but she wore a moon pendant, and virgins prayed to that goddess.

"No, I'm not."

Good. He tipped her chin up with his finger and stared into her eyes. "I want to worship your body. Will you let me?"

Allie couldn't believe her predicament. Dr. Paula must think she took her instructions very seriously. Damn Dr. Paula, and damn Kell, with his dark, serious eyes and chiseled good looks. She had a weakness for handsome men. It always ended in heartbreak and disaster for her. This would be no different. A one-night stand with a man from another time? She must be out of her mind. Well, she *did* have orders to do whatever needed to make Kell more comfortable.

She should struggle, pull back, act like a civilized woman.

People are watching!

Struggle! her brain said very sternly.

Surrender, giggled her body.

She couldn't fight. Her muscles resisted about as strongly as marshmallows when he tugged on her arm. Besides, she suddenly realized the idea of people watching didn't bother her. *Am I an exhibitionist?* She had never thought about it. And now the idea made her knees go weak.

He wrapped his arm around her waist and pressed her to his rock-hard chest. "Allie, I take you in the name of Kell." His mouth curved into a smile. "I have remembered my name. It is Kell, son of Bran, son of Orin. Kellorin Branson is the name I go by in my troop. I have led my men to many victories against the invaders from the north. I must have died in battle and this is the paradise promised to valiant warriors."

As he spoke he flexed his hips and rubbed his cock in sensuous circles across her belly. Its smooth, hot tip burned her skin through the thin leather of her dress. Rushes of heat and cold alternately washed over her, leaving her panting and totally incapable of speech. The most gorgeous man she'd seen in her life wanted her. All she wanted was to scream fuck me, and she didn't remember how to say that in any foreign language. *Think, Allie!*

To know. To know a woman meant to fuck her.

She stared at his perfect features—dark, burning eyes, high cheekbones and a long, narrow nose above full lips. Lips coming closer to her face and brushing her temples, her cheeks, branding slow kisses down her chin and over her throat.

"Know me," she begged, a sharp spasm shaking her belly and spearing her right through her cunt.

The idea that people watched sent shivers of excitement down her spine. Exhibitionist? You bet your sweet ass. Another flash of heat inundated her body. But only exhibitionist up to a point. She led Kell to one of the beds set into the wall and pulled the curtain closed.

The niche was deep and the bed was soft. Kell kneeled beside her and untied the laces that fastened her dress. He paused, apparently giving her time to think, then, when she didn't protest, pushed her dress down to her waist. Her breasts ached for his touch, and touch them he did. He took them in his hands, his calloused palms rough on her sensitive nipples. They hardened, lengthening and darkening, and he leaned down to take one in his mouth. Fiercely, he tugged on her nipple, sucking hard. Soft growls came from his throat and he pushed her onto her back. Still on his knees, he grasped her hips and pulled her to him. Crouching over her, he took his cock in one hand. With his other, he reached beneath her dress and found her pussy. One finger dipped into her and she clenched her buttocks as he stroked her softly. His finger crooked and he probed delicately into her wet folds.

"Pure maiden you are not, and your readiness coats my hand like honey." He groaned and nudged the tip of his cock into her. "Your heated cunt welcomes my shaft. By Damara, I know you, Allie."

He grabbed both her thighs and thrust his hips forward, sheathing himself in her in one smooth movement. His face darkened and he uttered a long, drawn-out growl. Like a wolf, he threw his head back and howled as he drove into her.

His raucous cry raised the hair on the back of her neck, while his wiry hands held her thighs wide. Her dress bunched around her waist and bared her pubic mound. His glistening cock sank between her labia, sliding, as if buttered, into her aching cunt.

He kneeled over her. The view he offered made her head spin. His muscular torso might have come from a Greek statue, stunning in its perfection. Her eyes followed the dark line of pubic hair, descending from his navel to his cock. Her labia hugged his root tightly, and thrust, his balls slapping lightly against her ass. His muscles flexed and he drove his cock deeper. The moment it hit her cervix a bolt of pleasure mixed with exquisite pain shot through her.

Slowly he drew out, letting just the tip of his cock tease her entrance. He grinned down at her. "Do you love that, my sweet Allie?"

"Yes." Gasping, she raised her hips, trying to spear herself on his hardness.

He only teased her more, flexing his buttocks so that his cock stroked her slick flesh, rubbing gently but insistently on her clit. A burning started in her pussy, spreading to her head, making her dizzy with desire so strong she thought she would scream or go crazy. And still his cockhead caressed her clit as he ignored her little cries of frustration. She lifted her hips, straining to catch his cock in her pussy.

He pushed her knees even wider and, with a strong thrust, buried himself to the hilt. A shock wave rippled through her body each time his cock hit her cervix. Her vision went dark. She thrashed back and forth, submerged by the sensations of pain and pleasure. Too deep, too strong, too good… Oh, God, it *felt good!* She dragged air into her burning lungs, gasping his name. "Kell!"

The pelts on the soft bed beneath her rubbed up and down her back when she moved, and her scalp tingled with static electricity. She dug her fingers into the fur, clutching as hard as she could.

His cock quivered inside her as he held himself perfectly still, his hands on her thighs, the tendons standing out on his neck. A loud groan rumbled in his throat and he unsheathed himself, her juices glistening on his cock. His breathing grew harsher and his hands trembled on her thighs, but his grip didn't lessen. He thrust into her, inch by inch, then with another deep growl he pulled out, resting his cock on her belly.

"No!" She wanted him inside her. She craved him so much it tore at her soul.

Her nipples ached and her breasts jiggled. She raised her hips, pushing against his hands. She might have been pushing steel girders. His fingers tightened, clutching her body to the point of pain.

Effortlessly, he held her immobile. Then, with a wolfish grin, he thrust into her, all his weight and strength behind his cock, impaling her right to her womb. Another starburst of pleasure-pain blinded her. She cried out, incapable of stopping herself. Her body convulsed and a tumult of throbbing seized her cunt. An orgasm stronger than any she had ever experienced ripped through her. Helplessly, she watched her belly contract. Her cunt clamped onto his cock and suddenly he tipped his head back and howled again, then he pulsed inside her. Stream after stream of hot seed hit her cervix, and it pushed her over the edge.

She heard herself screaming, harsh cries mingled with his roars, and as he collapsed on top of her, her last thought glimmered like a star in the darkness.

This man has waited over two thousand years for me.

Chapter Two

My name is Kellorin Branson. I have fought the invaders and chased them from my lands. I have traded with many people, even the barbarians from the Western forests, and I have traveled many leagues. I have seen different lands, learned much of men and beasts, but I know not where I am now, nor how I came to be here.

Kell looked at the woman sleeping on the furs. If he woke her, she might tell him what he wanted to know, but he was loath to disturb her slumber. A strong, protective feeling toward her surprised him. He had never imagined himself as particularly demonstrative. This one had changed all that. A smile tugged at his mouth as he stared at her. Small, strong, red-haired and fair-skinned like a true Celt, with wide hips and breasts made for sucking and kneading. Just the thought of touching her skin made his cock harden again. He stroked it absently, then he pulled back the curtain and looked around the room. He recognized some things. Others left him perplexed. Puzzles intrigued him. He remembered that much about his former life. He slid out of the bed and walked to the hearth.

One thing he noticed right away was the lack of odors in this place. His sensitive nose flared as he tested the air, but he smelled nothing familiar…except the rich, heady scent of the woman's sex and the sharper smell of his own seed. He was sticky and wanted to wash, but the other thing he had noticed was the absence of a door leading to the outside. How did one leave this dwelling? He quelled a prickle of fear and moved to inspect the walls. Familiar, yet strange, the logs seemed too perfect, fitting together without the usual chinks and drafts an old longhouse invariably had. For he recognized the dwelling as a longhouse, but that told him nothing. He could be anywhere from the Tenes kingdom to the far north where the invaders called Norsemen lived.

And what season could it be? The fire warmed the longhouse, but there should be eddies of cold air, the smell of old smoke and sweat. It could not be winter, because the longhouse was too warm. No frigid air seeped through the cracks in the wall. And it could not be summer, for no mosquitoes whined about the room and no moths fluttered in the firelight.

He stooped and touched the floor. Wide planks, evenly hewn and sanded, but where were the signs of wear? Everything seemed newly made. The fire pit in the middle of the room burned brightly, but the smoke rose to the roof and seemed to vanish. The logs were neatly placed, but there were few ashes. The woven blankets on the benches looked new. They were finely made, but the colors were not quite right. Animal skins lay about. He recognized wolf, deer and bear skins, but they didn't appear natural — the whole place just didn't feel lived in.

He went to the washing room to relieve and cleanse himself, then he sat near the fire and pulled up his knees, resting his chin on his arms. He could recall most of his life clearly now, but still, huge holes remained. He couldn't remember how he had died, and that upset him. This place could be paradise, but he doubted it. Men had made the objects he saw, but some things could have been made by the gods. The idea of a halfway place betwixt death and life seemed most likely. Some things were familiar, but others made no sense to him, such as the small piece of ice in the crack in the wall.

The ice intrigued him. The air was far too warm for ice. He took a look around but saw nothing sharp or pointed. His knife no longer hung at his waist. He had woken up nude, which hadn't worried him. Not having a knife did worry him. He stood and carefully studied the room. Benches covered with blankets, the sleeping niches that lined the walls — there was a stone fire pit, a stack of firewood, a few woven baskets and a pitcher and a cup of water. Everything was right for a longhouse, but not quite right.

Taking a piece of firewood, he tapped sharply on a hot rock from the fire pit and split off a sliver of stone. He teased the sliver out of the fire and waited for it to cool a bit. Then he used the stone to pry the piece of ice out of the wall, and he stared, perplexed, at the object in his palm. It glittered like ice but wasn't cold. And other things clung to it, little strands of colored yarn. He poked at it, trying to make sense of the object. A trickle of fear shivered down his spine but he didn't know why. Then a soft sound alerted him and he turned.

Allie opened her eyes. She had fallen asleep. The stress of flying had drained her, and her body still ached from Kell's lovemaking. She raised her head and searched for him. He stood by the wall, examining something in his hand. Something small and glittery.

Sudden panic shot her to her feet. Somehow he had pried the camera right out of the wall. If only he had done that sooner. A nervous giggle shook her. What must the scientists *think* of *me*? Who *cares*? She climbed out of the bed, pulled her dress on, and went to him.

He saw her coming and a smile lit up his face. She had never thought about that expression being literally true until now. His grin split his face and his eyes twinkled.

"Hail, Allie, did you have a good sleep?" he asked in Latin.

"Aye, thank you. Don't you prefer to speak Celtic?"

"It matters not. Look. What can this be?" He held out his hand, the remains of a tiny camera in it.

"What do you think it is?" she asked cautiously. What could she tell him? He would have to know sometime what had happened to him. A psychologist would come in handy right now.

He shook his head. "I have no idea. I believed it to be ice

at first, but now I see it is made of glass and some silver. I thought it might be copper too, but oddly melted. And this type of yarn I have never seen." He held up a tiny, plastic-covered wire. He appeared almost forlorn for a moment, then his expression hardened. "I had hoped you could tell me where I am, and how I died."

Allie sighed inwardly. The truth would be the best thing to tell him. At least, she hoped so. She nodded and patted the bench nearest the fire. "Come sit down next to me."

He did, his presence nearly overwhelming her. His scent filled her nostrils, acrid and male. He sat, his expression worried, waiting for her to speak.

"You set out in the wintertime, and you must have been on a journey far to the north. Do you remember any of that?"

He closed his eyes, his nostrils growing white as he drew a deep breath. Eyes still closed, he said, "I remember Tor shouting, and Vix crying out something about the ice breaking. We were farther north than we had ever been, but we were searching for something." His face twisted. "We were searching for women. Stolen by the invaders. Tor's wife. Vix's sister. Other women from our tribe. I do remember that much. But after Vix's cry, I know not what happened."

"You must have fallen into a crevice in the glacier and landed in water just on the verge of freezing solid." Pity lanced her heart. Everything he had known or loved was lost.

"Falling." He rubbed the bridge of his nose. "All is darkness around me, darkness and cold. Even when I woke up. Did I die?"

"You nearly died," whispered Allie. "But your body was found, and we...we woke you up."

"How is that possible? How can I awake after death, unless this is the afterlife and I am a shade? Am I a shade? Answer me." His eyes, the irises so dark brown as to appear almost black, beseeched her.

Allie took his hand and held it tightly. "No, you're not a shade. You are alive. In reality, you never died, not completely, anyway. You fell into a deep sleep caused by the cold, and our doctors woke you up."

His expression cleared. "So that is it! I am in the far north, and that is why everything looks strange. Tell me, where are Vix and Tor? I need to rejoin my companions so that we may search for our women."

A sharp pain tightened Allie's throat. How could she tell him? Her hesitation must have been eloquent, because he suddenly froze, his eyes clouding.

"They are dead, is that it?"

Miserably, she nodded. "Yes. I'm sorry. We never found them. And, Kell, I have to tell you something important. Listen."

But he stood, brushing her aside. "Perhaps I can find them on my own. Will your tribe help me? Are there warriors among your men willing to come with me to the land of the invaders to rescue the women?"

Mutely she stared at him, willing him to understand.

His body grew very still. "What is it? Do you know something about them too?"

"No." She wished he would sit down but he remained standing, superb and as completely unaware of his naked body as a wild animal. It distracted her but she had to tell him the terrible truth of his situation. "Sit, please."

Instead he paced back and forth. The impression she had of a wild animal grew stronger. He strode like a panther, or a wolf, each movement controlled and fluid. Then he turned to her, his face a mask of distress. "I never died, but my friends are lost as are the women we seek, is that right?"

"You slept for a long time, longer than you can ever imagine. Everyone you knew is gone, the world has changed and time...has passed you by." She faltered, unsure how to continue.

"I can imagine time better if you told me how long it has been since I fell into the ice." His voice raised goosebumps on her arms. "If the world has changed, tell me, are any of my tribe still left?"

"It has been more than two thousand years."

He missed a step. "What did you say?" His face turned ashen and he put his hand on the wall to steady himself. The remains of the camera fell on the floor and he looked at them. Wordlessly he kneeled and picked up the piece of wire, holding it as if it could bite. His hand trembled then stilled. Pale, he gazed at her, his eyes twin wells of bottomless pain. "For two thousand years I slept while my people lived and died? Are there any of my blood left?" A shudder racked him. "It matters not. I am alone. I understand that."

Allie wanted to tell him that he wasn't alone, that she was with him, but his eyes held so much grief she couldn't speak. The words stayed locked in her throat. Tears filled her eyes so that she could hardly see him.

Then the door opened a crack. Instantly, he whirled around, putting himself between her and the sliver of light that appeared. She put her hand on his arm, intending to tell him not to be afraid, when she heard a sharp crack. A red, plumed dart suddenly bloomed in his arm and he jerked but he didn't let go of her.

"What the...?" she gasped.

"Don't move! I'll protect you." He yanked the needle from his arm and she recognized a tranquilizer dart. *Why? What is going on?*

"Someone shoots strange arrows at us. How do we get out of here?" His voice slurred and he shook his head. "What happens to me? By Lugh, I see only darkness!"

Allie screamed as he sank to the floor, unconscious. "What is going on?" *Oh, God, don't let him be hurt. How can they do this to him?*

The door opened fully and she saw Dr. Paula and Captain Bide. The captain held a gun. Dr. Paula rushed in and seized Allie's arm.

"You poor thing! Raped by a savage! Come, I'm taking

you to the infirmary. We'll take care of you. Do you want a tranquilizer?"

Allie pulled her arm free. "Why did you shoot him?"

"He became violent. Then he pushed you into the bed and pulled the curtain closed so he could rape you!"

"We made love!" Allie had to clench her teeth so as not to scream again. "You did ask about his mating ceremonies, as I recall. How dare you shoot him? What do you think you're doing?"

Dr. Paula gaped at her. "I said ask about it, not actually participate in one!"

"If you thought he was raping me, why didn't you come charging in then, instead of waiting?" Allie was shocked and terrified. "What is going on? Why didn't you let me speak to him? He knows something is wrong. I told him he had slept for centuries."

The captain strode into the room and prodded Kell with his foot. "Well, he's sleeping some more. Let's put him in restraints. Then you can ask him the list of questions we prepared." He shoved a paper at Allie. "Don't show this to anyone else. That is an order. Come on, let's go, team."

Mr. Smith, flanked by three other men, came in and got Kell. They carried him away and into another room, this time all in white, with a table and fastenings. They strapped him down and stood guard by the door. Allie followed at their heels, panicked that Kell might wake up and find himself in such strange, modern surroundings.

"You shouldn't have him here," she said furiously, turning to Dr. Paula.

"He's proven that he can be dangerous. You poor thing! Come, let me take you to the infirmary," insisted Dr. Paula. She held up the bear-claw necklace. "You should have worn this. It would have made him respect you. I'm an anthropologist and I know what I'm talking about."

Allie wanted to stay with Kell but the scientists shooed her away. Damn! She glared at Dr. Paula. "Well, I hope you got all your notes straight about the mating ceremony."

"I have never been so embarrassed in my life," huffed Dr. Paula, two bright red spots appearing on her cheeks. "Luckily the curtain blocked most of the action. I couldn't watch. I let the men look. They certainly seemed to enjoy the show."

Allie wanted to choke the woman with her bear-claw necklace but she followed her to the showers without replying. It would do no good to start a fight. She would wash up and find out what they wanted with Kell. Something didn't seem right here. She clutched the paper Captain Bide had given her. Once alone in the showers, she read at it.

What year were you born? Where were you born? What languages do you speak? Did you go to school? Have you ever been to Russia? Do you work for the Russians? Have you heard of...?

Confused, Allie peered at the rest of the questions. Apparently the scientists believed that Kell worked for the Russians as a spy. Why they thought such a thing was beyond her, unless they hadn't told her everything.

After her shower, Mr. Smith came to get her. He took her to a cubbyhole of a room — an office with a fax machine and a computer — and coldly told her that she wouldn't be needed until the next day. "Tonight we'll be doing some physical experiments with the subject. Try to get some rest." He sneered.

"What makes you think he's a Russian spy?" She had never been one to hedge.

He narrowed his eyes. For a second she feared he wouldn't answer, but he did. "A team of Russian scientists found him. When we arrived, they gave up their discovery rather too quickly and it made us suspicious. Did you know the Russians have perfected the art of cryogenics? It's true. They planted this man in ice so that he could spy on us."

"But why?"

"We have discoveries and technologies that the Russians want. We've been trying to find out about cryogenics for ages. If he's real, we'll use his body to discover more about how the ice preserved his vital organs such as his brain. If he's a fake, he'll soon find he would have been better off back home."

"Who else believes he's a fake?"

"Captain Bide and I are sure he's a fake. Dr. Paula and her team of specialists hope he's for real. But whatever the truth is, it doesn't matter. He's our chance to study cryogenics and catch up with the Russians."

"What do you mean it doesn't matter? What are you going to do with him?"

He leaned against the doorway and gave her a calculating glance. Instinctively, she crossed her arms over her chest.

"Can you see him living in the modern world? If he is for real, he doesn't have a chance in a million to fit in anywhere. He would be a freak. Hell, he is a freak. And he's unpredictable and dangerous. Look what he did with you. He sees a woman and rapes her. Maybe that was fine in his time, but this is modern civilization. He won't fit in."

"So you're going to keep him here forever?" She blinked, still not wanting to believe what she heard.

"Until we get whatever information Dr. Paula wants about the Iron Age, which isn't much. Or until Captain Bide determines he really is a spy. But what is important to us is how he survived the big chill." The smile he gave her didn't reach his eyes. Then he spun on his heels and left her room.

As he left, a piece of fax paper fell from the desk and floated to the floor. Allie stopped to pick it up. As she did, some of the words caught her eye.

The subject has proven violent and uncontrollable. Dr. Paula says she doubts he can adapt to modern life if he really is from the past. As soon as she is finished studying him, and whether or not Captain Bide discovers if the subject is in fact a Russian spy,

I give my permission to terminate the subject since it seems that there is much to be learned from his brain tissue.

Who wrote this? She studied the name and phone number, but what she saw didn't tell her anything. Her skin crawled. Could it be that the scientists had never intended to keep Kell alive? Shivers ran down her back as she contemplated his words. *I give my permission to terminate the subject since it seems that there is much to be learned from his brain tissue...* Oh, God. They meant to dissect him. Whether he was from the past or not, it made no difference. Once they were done studying him, he would die. She had to think of a way to save him. Trembling, she stuffed the fax in her pocket.

A buzzer sounded then a voice came over a loudspeaker announcing dinner for the team in the cafeteria. Hesitantly, Allie left her room. She found the cafeteria and went inside, blinking in the harsh light. She picked up a tray but all there was to eat were servings of anemic salad and sliced turkey with gravy. Her appetite had fled, but she picked at her food. The team of scientists and military personnel trickled in to eat. Captain Bide sat on the opposite side of the room from Dr. Paula, Allie noted. Mr. Smith came in, hesitated, and joined her.

"Getting acclimated?" he asked.

Allie took a bite of her turkey. It might as well have been sawdust. "Well, it's not the Ritz."

He gave a surprised laugh. "I never would have pegged you for someone with a sense of humor."

I never would have pegged you for a murderer, she thought. She took another bite of turkey. "What will my schedule be like?"

"That's up to Captain Bide and Dr. Paula. They are in charge of the operation. I'm leaving tomorrow. But don't worry, they won't need you tonight. The dose of tranquilizer he got will keep him knocked out all night long." He hesitated. "I'm surprised at your reactions here. You didn't go to pieces like most women would have. You acted like a real pro. We could use someone like you in our CIA program."

She didn't answer, too busy thinking of the implications of what he had said. If a woman didn't scream and cry, it surprised him. If she stabbed him with a fork would he be surprised too? Because that's what she wanted to do to him right now.

He wiped his lips with his napkin and gave her a look. She definitely didn't like his expression. His next words confirmed her worst fears. He put his hand on her arm and said, "I couldn't help seeing what happened today. It must have been quite...brutal." His voice dropped to a murmur. "If you'd like, I can stay with you tonight, help erase that... nightmare and replace it with something gentler." He took her hand and placed it where his hard-on pressed against his pants.

Okay, first I'll stab him in the heart with a fork then I'll saw off his balls with my butter knife. "No, thank you. I've had enough excitement for one day." She stood and grabbed her tray. *Should I drop it on his lap?* Her fingers itched to let it go, but she managed to smile coolly and leave the room without creating a scene. She had to make a plan. But first she needed to see Kellorin.

No guards in front of his door. Nothing. She peeked inside. He lay on a bed, strapped down, and still, thank God, unconscious. She couldn't bear to think of him waking up and finding himself in this predicament. There was a folding chair in the corner of the room. She pulled it to the side of his bed and sat next to him, stroking his hand.

She didn't see him move. Without warning, he grabbed her wrist and held it like a steel trap.

"What is this place?" he said, his voice completely lucid. He opened his eyes and stared at her. "Where am I?"

She swallowed hard, her heart pounding. "You should still be asleep."

"Speak to me. Tell me why I'm tied like a wild animal." His eyes were pleading.

She looked at the door then back at him. "How do you feel?"

"I feel hunger."

"I'll bring you some food." She put her hand on his, and he relaxed enough for her to slide her wrist from his grip. "If anyone else comes in here, you must pretend to be asleep. Do you understand?"

"I understand your words but not your reason. You speak but you do not answer my questions." He pulled fruitlessly against his bonds then slumped back on the bed, his chest heaving.

"The people here want to study you, to find out how you survived for so long asleep in the ice. Some believe you come from...your time. Others..." She grimaced, not sure how to explain. "They are convinced you are trying to trick them."

"And you? What do you think?"

She put her finger to her lips. "I hear someone coming. I believe you. I will help you. Please, trust me."

He flashed her a wry grin. "What choice do I have? I am bound and helpless."

The door opened. Dr. Paula entered and raised her eyebrows. "You shouldn't be here."

"I was afraid he'd wake up and be frightened." Allie looked at Kell. He lay still, his eyes closed, his hands slack, in all appearances asleep. For a second she almost thought she had hallucinated, but her wrist was still faintly red where he had grabbed her. "Where are the guards?"

"Guards?" Dr. Paula shook her head. "What guards?"

"You know, men or women with high-powered assault rifles standing around watching everyone carefully in case someone tries to esc— I mean, break in and steal the ice man."

The doctor's face cleared and she shrugged. "We had guards while they built the longhouse to keep the workers away from the laboratory where we kept the ice man. But what do we need guards for now? We're in the middle of nowhere. The ice man can't escape. He's very firmly strapped down, and when we do let him go, he'll be in the longhouse with you, where we'll watch him constantly with cameras. As for someone breaking in, first they have to get by our security perimeter controlled from the office. It's an electric fence guaranteed to fry anyone or anything that touches it."

"I'm so reassured." Allie managed a brave smile.

"He won't be wake until tomorrow. Why don't you go get some sleep? Be here at eight a.m. and that way you can comfort him when he does wake up. And don't forget the necklace this time." Dr. Paula smiled and patted her arm. "I'll stay here with him. Go back to your room and get a good rest, Allie."

"Goodnight." Allie went to her little room and sat on her bed. *How much time do I have? When are they going to...kill him?* She had to save him. She couldn't live with herself if she let anything happen to him.

Chapter Three

Kell lay on his bed and, from beneath lowered lashes, studied the woman in the room with him. She didn't resemble his Allie. This woman had a sharp face, all angles and edges. Her eyes reminded him of a bird's — quick, darting and frightened. *Do I frighten her?*

She wore a long white robe with strange fastenings in the front, and she carried a sort of tablet, writing on it with a stylus every once in a while. She would peer at him, then write, then look at him again and write some more. It made him nervous.

The bed beneath him was smooth and soft, and the covers lay lightly upon his body yet kept him very warm. Too hot, even. The room was small and the air stuffy and bland. He hated everything about it. The white walls were perfectly straight, unadorned, and far too bright. They dazzled his eyes. The strange, tube-shaped fire globe that lit the room hurt his eyes, as well, and cast a light that reminded him of winter sunlight on blinding snow. But the air bothered him the most. It had a metallic tang that made his head ache. Gone were the familiar smells of smoke and sweat, the reassuring scent of pine and lavender used to freshen the rooms, and the spicy scent of peppermint and borage he remembered...

Stop. Stop *thinking of all that.* He had almost lost control of himself and given in to his grief as sorrow hit him afresh. He quieted his spirit and dared another look at the woman in the room. She studied her tablet, a frown on her face. She still believed him asleep. He relaxed, tension seeping from him slowly as he tried to put his memories in order.

He, Kellorin, son of Bran, had lived on the island of Tu'Og near the coast of the Greater Island. Educated in his tribe by the elders and the druid master, he had traveled to the warm waters of the Inner Sea, where the Greeks and Phoenicians plied their boats and traded amphorae of wine for his pine pitch. He had voyaged to the north where the Norsemen made their longhouses, and to the southwest in Iberia, where the men wore their hair in long spikes and tattooed their faces. He had even traded with the mighty lords of the Tenes kingdom, admiring their impressive stone fortresses.

He hadn't lived in a fortress. He had lived in a comfortable house, with an entranceway, cloakroom, main living room, sauna and herb garden. His wife, Wodicca, had tended that garden until she'd taken to bed in childbirth and had died, the babe with her.

Afterward, he had continued to trade, to travel, to live, but something had been broken inside him. Then one day invaders had come from the north. The raiders had sought women for their tribe, and they'd stolen three women who had been washing clothing at the river's edge—Tor's wife and daughter, and Vix's sister. The men had asked him to accompany them on their quest to free them, and he had agreed, sharpening his dagger and loading his quiver with arrows.

Their journey had led them north to the land of unending ice and snow…and there his journey had ended. Only to resume two thousand years later. He clenched his fists, but he gave no other sign of his torment. He had left everything he'd known and loved behind, but he lived in the here and now…wherever that was.

The only spark of hope in this place was Allie. She had mended whatever had broken when his wife had died. Now, instead of hopeless darkness, there was warm sunshine.

Allie. He whispered her name to himself and closed his eyes, ignoring the hunger pains gnawing at his belly. She would come to him again, and he would claim her as his own. They would never part.

* * * *

Allie opened her suitcase and shook out her clothes. Her heart sank. Nothing would be suitable for what she wanted to do. She set aside all her socks and underwear, her stockings and her woolen sweater. Putting her head in her hands, she thought hard. There must be a supply room in the hangar. After all, the soldiers working the runway had snowsuits and were equipped with outdoor clothing. She checked at her watch. Almost midnight. She had better move now. She opened the door to her room and looked both ways down the narrow corridor. No one seemed to be around.

The hangar was still flooded with bright light, but there were no sentries posted, Kell had been drugged and tied up and they were miles from anywhere, so apparently he wasn't being guarded. But Dr. Paula had mentioned something about an electrified security perimeter. She would have to do something about that. First she went to the office room where the fax machine was located. On the wall she had also noticed a fuse box. Inside it she found different fuses clearly marked. Garage, longhouse, cafeteria, showers… security — *That's the one.* She pulled out the fuse and closed the box.

Next she went to the supply room, which was indicated by a large orange sign. Nice of them to be so organized and mark everything so clearly visibly. She found two snowsuits and two backpacks already filled with survival kits and ready to go. She hesitated then took a knife and carefully slashed the rest of the snowsuits to ribbons. She couldn't risk having the guards on her heels too soon. Now, in order to follow them, they would have to get new outfits. She stuffed the two snowsuits she had taken into a large garbage bag, hefted the backpacks onto her shoulders, and went in search of food.

In the kitchen, she grabbed up as much butter and cheese as she could find, along with chocolate, powdered soups, coffee, sardines and salami. Fat. They would need fat. The cold burned calories and dehydrated people. She found a box of water-purifying tablets and put it in one of the packs along with everything else. It was starting to get heavy. Then she made two sandwiches with lots of butter and salami. These were for Kell. Feeling a bit like a mule, she carried the baggage, sandwiches and the two snowsuits to his room. As she suspected, no one stood guard — everyone slept.

Except Kell. He saw her as she staggered into the room, and a smile lit up his eyes, although his mouth gave only the faintest of twitches. She tossed the snowsuits to the floor, put the sacks down and placed his sandwiches on his bed.

"Ave, Allie," he said gravely.

"Ave, Kell." She untied him and waited until he'd finished eating.

"'Tis good food," he said. "The bread is tender and the meat well spiced."

"Here, drink this." She gave him a bottle of water.

He examined the plastic bottle for what seemed a long time, running his hands over it, staring at it. Finally, he lifted it to his lips and drank. "The water has a strange taste," he said with a frown.

She didn't know what to say. When she was close to him her body reacted in a most primitive way. Her nipples stiffened, her body remembered the feel of his cock sliding into her, and her face flushed.

He finished drinking and turned to her, his eyes searching. "Where are we going?"

"You know that we're leaving?" She had been sure she'd have to explain everything.

He pointed to the bag. "That sack is full, and you untied me and fed me, so I think you have the intention of taking me somewhere. Where are we going?" he repeated patiently.

She picked up the snowsuits. She had also found pants, socks and clothes for him. They would find boots in the store room. She gave him everything and he dressed slowly, taking his time to examine each item. The elastic in all the material gave him pause, but he said nothing, just raised his eyebrows a bit. When he was dressed, she put on her snowsuit and he imitated her. Velcro straps were unfamiliar, and so were zippers, but his hands were deft, and he had an uncanny ability to imitate gestures perfectly. She only had to show him something once.

Once they were both dressed, he took her face in his hands and bent, pressing his lips softly against hers. "Thank you," he whispered.

Her knees buckled, but she managed to stay upright and not drag him to the floor and strip off all his clothes. They didn't have the time. She scanned the area. The coast was clear. She motioned for him to follow her.

He stepped out of the door and froze. His eyes widened as he took in the size of the building. She could see his gaze moving up the walls, along the struts, to the arched ceiling so far above. A muscle twitched in his jaw and a shudder ran through him.

"Are you all right?" she whispered.

He nodded, the color draining from his face. He saw the longhouse, built in the middle of the hangar, and a strange expression filled his eyes.

"What is it?" she asked, tugging softly on his sleeve.

"Is that where I woke up?" He pointed to the longhouse.

"Yes. The scientists built it so you wouldn't feel out of place."

He gave her a level glance. "I am out of place here, no matter where I am. Tell me, what are those vines growing along the roof?"

"They aren't vines—they're wires where electricity runs. They carry the light and the..." She frowned, not sure how to explain. "They carry voices too. We can communicate from great distances because some wires carry sound as well as light."

He stood still, his face turned toward the ceiling. "There are torches that give more light than the sun, up there, and I see flames captured in glass." He pointed to the naked light bulbs strung along a wire. "I see nothing I recognize, except the building I woke up in. Everything else, even the floor, is strange to me. Does everyone live in such a huge, empty house now? Where are your villages?"

"This isn't a dwelling. It's a station built especially to study you."

His eyebrows rose. "Me? Why?"

"Can we talk about this later? We have to leave now. Please?" Allie looked at her watch. One a.m. They had to get out of the hangar before someone caught them.

He put his backpack on and followed her, walking so silently that twice she turned to make sure he was still behind her. In the store room, they put on boots, and Allie found the keys to the garage above ground where they kept the snowmobiles. She took all the keys hanging in the cabinet and led the way to the lift.

She saw Kell flinch hard when the lift started to move, and the skin on his face tightened. But he said nothing, and, as they rose above the floor, he carefully scanned the room as if searching for something.

They left the hangar without any trouble. As Allie suspected, no guards had been posted. When they stepped out of the door, the icy wind slapped at them. Allie was glad of the furred hood covering most of her face. Although it might nearly be spring, winter still had this land in its tight grip. Taking Kell's hand, she made her way through the dark toward the small rounded building near the doorway. To her relief it was the garage.

She opened the door and they slipped inside. She hit the lights. Five snowmobiles were lined up. She checked the gas tanks. Full and ready to go. Each snowmobile had an extra can of gas. She took as many as she could carry and strapped them on one snowmobile. She tried the keys she had found in the office until she found the one that started the snowmobile nearest the exit. She stuffed the other keys in her pocket. There were maps tacked on the wall. As she studied at them her heart pounded and her head spun. She hadn't even thought of bringing a map. She carefully unpinned one from the wall. Kell leaned over her shoulder.

"What is that?"

"It's a map. It tells us where we are." She showed him the small square marking the base. "We have to go here in order to find shelter." She pointed to the east, toward the coast, where she hoped to find a village.

He nodded, his expression bleak. She supposed she understood. Everything he knew was useless now. He would have to learn everything all over again, and it must be bewildering.

Then she got on the snowmobile and told Kell to sit behind her and hold on tightly. He did, wrapping his powerful arms around her waist. She started the snowmobile, thanking her lucky stars that her cousins had one and she'd driven it often. With the map in her pocket and the compass on her wrist, she drove out of the garage and into the night. She stopped at the security fence at the gate near the garage, but she had shut the electricity off, and she opened the gate with no trouble.

If all went as planned, they would have at least a six-hour head start.

Chapter Four

Kell nodded, his eyes burning with sleep. Beneath him, the machine that ran across snow rumbled steadily, eating up the leagues, putting distance between them and his prison. Sometimes he could believe that he dreamed, that the darkness and the cold were only part of his dream. He would wake, and Vix would laugh at him, his eyes crinkling with mirth. Vix always laughed…

He shook his head and tightened his arms around Allie's waist. The woman was strong. Strength was something he admired in a woman, and she rode the machine with an ease that astounded him and made him a wee bit jealous. The terrain rose and fell, trees loomed out of the darkness, but the machine had a glowing eye that cast a beam of light and showed them the way.

Did Allie follow the light or did she direct it? How did the machine move with no wheels and no legs? He hadn't gotten a good look at it in the stables where they had been kept. He had seen things but didn't understand them yet. At first, he had assumed the row of machines was all one entity, but then Allie had explained they were like chariots and were used for transportation. Of course, then he had wondered where the horses were kept. When Allie had brought the machine to life it had roared like a dragon, and he'd nearly jumped out of his skin. He had found himself with his back pressed against the wall, his hands digging into the wood.

Thankfully Allie hadn't noticed, and he'd managed to peel himself off the wall before she had motioned to him to approach. He had forced his legs to move, praying she didn't see how terrified the machine made him.

He had recognized some things, like the many doors and windows inside that strange white prison. But he hadn't been able to comprehend the tangled web of vine-like metal strung about. And though he had seen many different kinds of dwellings in his life, he'd yet to see one made of metal, like his prison.

Stop. He didn't want to go there anymore. Instead he watched the light as it stabbed into the darkness, but his eyes stung and his head still ached with sleep. Another gust of wind whipped stinging snow particles across his cheeks and he narrowed his eyes. Now, in the light, snow swirled thickly, obscuring their route. Allie slowed the machine to a crawl. For a while they continued like that, making their way blindly into the snowstorm. But suddenly a tree seemed to come out of nowhere, and Allie barely swerved the machine in time. She stopped and leaned over, exhaustion written on her face.

Kell glanced up at the sky. No sign of dawn, and, in the light of the machine's eye, snow fell in a thick curtain. But the fir tree in front of them leaned invitingly, its sweeping branches already heaped with snow. Kell got off the machine and ducked under the branches. A space between the trunk and the branches beckoned. Perfect. He motioned to Allie, who nodded, pointing toward the machine. She wanted to put it under the branches as well.

First they took their supplies off it. Then they hid the machine under the largest branch, creating a windbreak for them as well.

Kell nodded in satisfaction, but when the machine stopped, so did the light. Then Allie took a short, thick stick out of her bag and a beam of light shot from it, startling him. She propped it in a fork in the branches and started to set up a small, round tent. He watched her, his muscles tensing as she worked, imitating her moves in his head. The tent was familiar in shape. He had seen similar tents in the steppes, but those had been made of skins, while this one seemed made of moonbeams. It shimmered, but when he touched it, it was slippery like the smooth skin of some strange fish. Could it be eel skin?

Allie looked at him and pointed to the tent. "It's ready. Can you take the flashlight?"

He approached the light stick carefully and put his hand in front of it. No heat. It shone with a cold, clear light. Gingerly, he took the light out of the branch. He swung it around, pointing the light everywhere, seeing how far the beam traveled, marveling. He turned it to his face and blinked. The light was too strong and it hurt his eyes. *Amazing!* The wind moaned and whistled in the treetops, the storm building to a fever pitch. Before he crawled into the tent, Kell took a last look around, satisfying himself that the tent would be sheltered by the tree and the machine that ran over snow.

Inside the tent, Allie shrugged out of her snowsuit and hung it over a thin rope. Kell did the same, nodding his approval. In the cold, clothes had to be kept dry. He was amazed at how warm and dry the snowsuit and boots had kept him so far. Spacious and practical, the tent boasted a double door, a clothesline, and a small brazier that Allie wasted no time setting up. Kell sat still, his eyes taking in her every move. As before, some things seemed familiar, while others made no sense.

The brazier had a collapsible tube that fit into a hole in the tent. That made sense since smoke was a problem for tents. This brazier was made of white metal and stood on three sturdy legs. All that he had seen before. But this brazier had another, smaller tube that ran from the brazier to a small blue jug. The jug had a handle that turned, and a blue flame sprang from the top of the brazier so suddenly that Kell flinched.

Allie turned and patted his arm. "I'm sorry. All this must seem so strange to you."

He closed his eyes. Strange was not the word. Everything he had known had become twisted and bizarre. Familiar things had mutated into frightening machines. Even horses had turned into rumbling machines that belched stinking fog and had one bright eye. No, that was untrue. He knew what was machine and what was alive. His world had its share of machines, but none that ran by themselves. A shiver ran over his body.

Blindly, he put out his hand toward the warmth of the brazier. Fire still gave warmth. His hand brushed against soft skin and he froze.

Eyes still closed, he ran his fingertips over Allie's brow, over her cheeks and across her jaw. He drew a line with his fingers, following her neck to where her pulse beat strongly. She caught his hand in hers, holding it tightly. Pulling her to him, he pressed his lips to the soft skin on her temple. Her curly hair tickled his face, but he didn't open his eyes. The feel of a woman…that hadn't changed. The scent and taste of women hadn't changed.

A deep sigh escaped him as warmth crept into his bones. Soft and sweet, and strong and brave. "Allie," he whispered. The tent leaned, buffeted by the wind, but the brazier warmed the air, and he opened his eyes to stare at the woman who had saved him from the prison.

"What is it?" Her big brown eyes were questioning. Her lashes cast jagged shadows on her cheeks.

"Thank you." He slipped his hand behind her neck and pulled her to him.

A little hesitantly, she put her arms around his shoulders.

"You've got such broad shoulders," she said, a catch in her voice.

He tugged at her chemise and lifted it over her head, then stopped, perplexed. He had seen brassieres like hers in Rome, but they'd been made of knitted wool. This one was made of silk that stretched like a supple skin. She took it off, a smile curving her lips. Then she stood and slipped off her pants. In the pale, blue light of the brazier, her skin took on the glow of polished marble.

"You look like the statue of a nymph." He got to his knees

and cupped her buttocks in his hands. Holding her tightly, he pressed his face to her sex, letting the smell and feel of her soothe his shattered nerves.

She whimpered softly and leaned into him, allowing her legs to part slightly.

Tilting her pelvis with his hands, he nuzzled her pubis, lapping at her slit. His cock hardened when his tongue found her cleft and parted her labia, searching. Hot, slick flesh surrounded his tongue, and he thrust gently, stroking her until with a cry she opened for him, her rich juices making him so stiff he could hardly bear it.

He loved the taste of a woman, and Allie was like sweetest ambrosia. He found her clit with his tongue and flicked it hungrily, nibbling with his lips until she writhed in his hands, her gasps and mews growing louder as she got wetter.

He tightened his hands on her buttocks, squeezing her flesh. By Toutatis, he needed to fuck her now. He plunged his tongue one last time into her cunt then leaned back and tipped his head up, licking a trail from the inside of her thighs to her chest as he got from his knees to his feet. Sucking hungrily on each nipple, he reached for his cock.

Allie fit into his embrace perfectly. Two thousand years hadn't changed the way a woman fit into a man's arms. Another tremor ran through him. *Time, don't think about time.* The druids said it didn't exist, that it could be bent... They had been right.

He pushed his cock into her hot, tight sheath, and his buttocks clenched with each thrust. Little cries came from Allie's throat, exciting him more. He answered her with deep growls from his chest, his growls becoming louder as his balls contracted and pressure built in his groin.

Drawing his cock out of her sex, he gently lowered her to the floor. Kell admired Allie for a moment, his gaze roaming over the wealth of her curves, coming to rest on her face. She reached toward him, her face flushed. With a contented sigh, he plunged back into the snug warmth of her body.

Allie wrapped her legs around him, urging him with her heels drumming against his flanks. The hard thump of her heels, and her nails, raking across his back, spurred him on.

Suddenly a hot stream of seed shot from his cock, spurting into her womb with a force that nearly made him black out. He clasped her to him, holding on tightly, her breasts crushed to his chest as he emptied himself into her, feeling as if his life force left him as well. His arms trembled, and he breathed in great gulps. Allie shivered in his arms, her body still except for a slight tremor he could feel in her cunt, as if she milked the last of his seed into her body.

* * * *

Allie came to with the sound of the wind screaming in her ears. The tent rocked alarmingly, and gusts of wind deformed the walls, batting against it like the paws of some great beast. Cold had seeped in, but the Bunsen burner kept it at bay. She had set it on low to economize the butane. The tent had been designed for survival in the far north. Insulated from the floor to the roof, it would withstand even the most extreme temperatures.

Kell lay curled up and asleep in the corner, his head resting on his rolled-up sleeping bag. Allie opened her backpack and took out a washcloth, small pan and a bottle of water. She put the water in the pan and set it on the little stove to heat up. When it began to steam, she poured some onto the cloth and, shivering a bit in the chill, she washed herself before pulling on her clothes.

A glance at her watch told her it was just after three a.m. There was nothing else to do now except wait out the storm and hope the compass she had been following that night hadn't steered them wrong. She had headed northeast, toward a series of deep coves that scalloped the coastline. Hopefully the scientists would think they had headed south, toward the cities.

Kell didn't cease to impress her. Aside from an evident nervousness, he hadn't let on that anything had frightened him. He had sat upon the snowmobile and hadn't moved, although for the first few minutes he'd gripped her so tightly she had barely been able to breathe. He had been startled by the tent and the Bunsen burner, but aside from the materials they were made from, the objects wouldn't be that different from the shelters and braziers from his time period. What most people didn't realize was that nothing was new — everything had already been invented by the ancients. Modern man had simply improved on the design.

She glanced at her wristwatch. Well, electronic things and fuel-powered engines would be very new and different to Kell. So would little things like zippers and doorknobs. But ancient myths had mechanical beings in them, flying machines and, if you studied the mythology of the Celts and the Mayas, they even had theories about time being slowed, speeded up or even stopped altogether. So Kell wouldn't be too terribly overwhelmed if they could find a small, secluded village. She would help him adapt and find a place for himself, then she'd... She blinked. She had no idea what she'd do. She had put off thinking about the future as much as possible, but she had to face it sometime.

How could she leave Kell and go back to her life before? Would they arrest her? Fire her? Her head ached and she rubbed her temples. She would worry about all that later. Right now, she had to concentrate on Kell. Helping him find a new life seemed essential. Her heart contracted at the idea of leaving him, but they couldn't stay together forever. He deserved to be able to make his own life.

She could always go back and get a good lawyer. What could they do to her? She would have to pay for the snowmobile and the snowsuits that she'd ruined, and knowing the Army, the bill would be astronomical. But put her in prison? For what? They wouldn't want anyone to know that they had been about to dissect a living man. She had kept the fax. If the worst came to the worst, she could always use that for her defense.

But all that paled to finding Kell a place to live, where he could start over again. She glanced at him. He didn't appear cold, but she used the second sleeping bag to cover him. Then she made herself a coffee with the rest of the hot water and listened to the sound of the storm. Who would come after them, and how could she hide Kell?

Where would he be comfortable? *Could* he live in a city? She doubted it. How could he work? He had no identity. And what could he do? She put her arms around her knees and rocked back and forth. She had saved Kell, but was it really saving him? *Out of the frying pan, into the fire*, came to mind.

The best thing to do now would be to get him as far from the base as possible and try to get a human rights lawyer involved. The United Nations? Was she being ridiculous? Maybe a lawyer could help, but if Kell and she were caught before they could reach someone to help them, it would be game over. They would kill Kell, and since legally he didn't exist, they wouldn't even have to face charges. She could never prove Kell had existed. And even if she did find help, she had to stay hidden for as long as possible until it was proven publicly that he had been resuscitated from the ice, and was, in fact, from the past.

Exhaustion made her head spin and she tried desperately to sleep, but worries gnawed at her, and when dawn came, she was still in a fitful state between wakefulness and slumber.

Chapter Five

Riiiinnnngg!

Bruce Steele hit his night table with his hand but missed the telephone. Groaning, he sat up. His head ached and he rubbed his temples. Whatever he'd had last night hadn't let him off easy. The drink still hammered at his head. Or was it the noise of the damn phone?

Riiiinnnngg!

He cursed and fumbled for the light switch then regretted it as the light sent stabbing pains to his head. Eyes screwed shut, he grabbed his phone and flicked it on.

"What is it?" he growled.

"Bruce Steele?"

"Who is this?" His voice grated like splintered glass but his head had cleared instantly. He opened his eyes and squinted at the clock. Five a.m. "What do you want?"

"My name is Captain Bide. You don't know me and I have never met you, but I know all about you, Mr. Steele. And what I know is you're the man I need for my mission. I'll fill you in when you get here. I won't say anything over the phone. Be at the Montreal airport in two and a half hours, with your tracking—"

"Hold it, buddy. I don't remember giving you permission to call me, and I don't remember giving any indication I would track anyone this week. So why don't you just hang up right now and forget you ever called me."

"Mr. Steele, I don't think you understand me. I work for the United States government and we need your help. Your regular pay will be doubled."

Steele let his breath out slowly. Captain Bide, whoever he

was, had touched a nerve. "Triple it, and we have a deal."

"Done."

No hesitation. He should have held out for more. "All right, you have yourself a tracker. What flight am I on?"

"Go to Bear Lake Charters and tell them your name. Your plane leaves in three hours. You'll be here by ten a.m. and I'll fill you in then."

"Where exactly is here? I need to know…"

"You don't need to know anything right now. You'll find out everything when you get here."

"Fine, whatever you say." Steele clicked off his phone and stood, rubbing his hand over his face. An aspirin, a shower, a coffee, then he would grab the bag he always kept packed in case of emergencies like this and head out. Had some tourist gotten lost again? No, the government wouldn't be concerned about tourists. A soldier gone AWOL? Hell, maybe a whole platoon.

He took his coffee out of the microwave and sipped it as he studied the weather reports on the television. He was headed north, that much he could guess. He'd heard of Bear Lake charters. They serviced a large area up in Inuit country. He examined the weather patterns carefully, noting a large depression and storm warnings. Whoever had gotten lost had picked a very bad time to wander out into the wilderness.

A glance at his watch told him he had better hurry. He took his bag then made sure the house was locked tight. Before he drove off, he took the note he'd written and slid it in his neighbor's mailbox. Jed had a copy of his keys and would take care of the place for however long he was away. They'd had an agreement for years now.

Snow had started to fall when he reached the airport, and by the time he had gotten settled in the small twin-engine plane, it was coming down in thick flurries, driven by a chill wind. The plane bucked and dipped while it climbed, but Steele had never been afraid of flying, and he just held the overhead strap and stared out of the window when the plane finally broke out of the clouds and rose above the storm.

* * * *

The quiet woke Kell. The wind had stopped and deep silence had settled over everything. Opening his eyes, he saw by the soft light penetrating the top of the tent that it was full daylight. He sat up and looked around. Allie sat near the brazier. Their eyes met and she grinned. He couldn't help grinning back.

"How was your rest?" She handed him a bowl full of steaming soup and a spoon.

He took it and sipped carefully. "I had a good rest. Mmm. This is delicious. What is it?"

She raised her eyebrows. "It's only an instant soup — cream of potato. Oh, that's right. You wouldn't know a potato if it bit you on the ass."

"Are potatoes dangerous beasts?" He'd never had anything like this. He would have assumed it was a sort of vegetable mixed with flour. He sniffed at it and took another sip. "It doesn't taste like meat."

Allie burst out laughing. "A potato is a vegetable. They just didn't get to Europe until after your time."

He sipped his potato soup and considered her words. "Where did they come from? Where are we exactly?"

Allie set down her bowl and took a paper from her pocket. She unfolded it and showed it to him. "This is a map of the world. I took it when we were on the base. I wanted to show it to you."

There was nothing he recognized, but she patiently explained, starting with the Inner Sea, which she called the Mediterranean. Then she showed him Gaul — or France — and Iberia, which she called Spain. The British Isles he recognized, and with a flash of sudden comprehension, he traced the coastline north with his finger.

"The Tenes are here."

"Yes, that's Norway, and farther up is the land of glaciers and ice, where the scientists found your body." She paused then pointed. "The Atlantic Ocean you know is here. And these two continents are North and South America, discovered long after your time. We are now here, in this part of the world."

It all looked unfamiliar, but he peered closely, then put his finger on the map and said, "This is the island of endless ice."

She looked surprised.

"Our people know it. We trade for furs there."

"Have you been there?"

"Of course, I'm a trader." He shrugged and finished his soup. "I like potatoes." The silence settled once more over the tent and he cocked his head to listen. "The wind has fallen and we're covered with snow. Shall I dig us out? We can't stay here forever."

"All right. I'll pack up. If we go straight east now, we should come to the coast in a day or so. But we have to be careful because they will certainly be searching for us. The Army and the scientists will do anything to get you back." She suddenly started to tremble.

"But why? Why do they seek us? Why do they want me?" He couldn't wrap his mind around the fact that they were being hunted like beasts.

"Because you slept in the ice for so long, and they want to know how you did it."

He pulled on the clothes she had given him, his hands lingering on the strange material. "I have no idea how I did it, so I can be of no help to them. You can just tell them."

Her expression grew even more frightened. "They don't want to hear about it. They want to study your body to see how the cold affected it, and especially your brain." She tapped her skull.

"What does my brain have to do with anything?"

"Because they believe it can tell them how you slept so long. They want the information it can give them."

"Why? My brain? All my intelligence and spirit reside in my heart, everyone knows that." He wanted to take the fear from her eyes. "No, don't say anything. I will learn how to manage the metal beast, and I will take you to safety."

They dug out of the snow and packed the tent. Allie showed Kell how the metal beast worked. She called it a snowmobile. He had started to ask her for words in her language. Allie looked at the horizon and shivered.

"What is it?" he asked, putting his mittened hand on her shoulder.

"The wilderness is so vast here, and so dangerous. It frightens me. I'm not used to being so far from towns or cities." She turned her gaze to him, her dark eyes full of disquiet.

To him, it was home. "This place reminds me of my world. I loved to travel in the far north. The land of endless ice was one of my favorite places to go. Perhaps we can make our way there and settle, but you would be too cold. Perhaps there is a place that has ice for me, and fire for you. Is there a land of ice and fire?"

She looked startled. "Yes, there is. It's an island called Iceland. Why didn't I think of that?"

He imagined a place near the ocean, a small dwelling where they could be together. "I will learn your language, and you can show me your world."

Allie nodded. "We have to get to the coast. There will be boats heading to Iceland, for sure. Why not? And we can apply for political asylum." She patted the snowmobile and motioned for him to sit in front of her. "If you want to learn to drive, put your hands on mine and watch."

Kell found it easy to learn to ride the snowmobile, but not as easy to judge its speed. Twice they nearly tipped over. But he prided himself on his riding ability and wasn't about to let a noisy machine get the better of him. "I hate the sound it makes," he complained, shaking his head to clear the buzzing from his ears.

"We can't do much about that, I'm afraid."

"You have invented a wonderful machine, but you have given it a terrible voice. Why can't it run quietly, like the wind? How can you sneak up on your prey with this?"

"We don't need to hunt for food anymore. Animals are raised in huge farms and slaughtered for meat, and farmers grow vast fields of wheat for bread. Everything is sold in markets all over the world, and hardly anyone has to go out to hunt."

Kell digested this bit of information. "So everyone lives like the Romans now? Heating in their houses, food in the markets, running water right to the apartment buildings."

"Did you go to Rome?"

"Of course." Kell nodded. "I went there often."

"Did you?" She sounded impressed, and well she should. Rome awed everyone who saw her.

"The first time I set foot in the city, I couldn't believe such a place existed. The tallest buildings I'd ever seen towered overhead, and the crowded streets never emptied until nightfall. Chariots thundered down the streets, and wagons loaded with goods came from all over the world. The port of Ostia teemed with boats, and the river jammed with barges and boats as traders arrived at the docks."

"Did you arrive by boat then?"

"Yes, and I went back several times afterward. Each time Rome seemed to grow bigger." It helped to remember Rome, because his arms, legs and head ached with the noise and vibration of the snowmobile. His stomach growled and he realized he was famished.

"We should set up camp soon. When night falls we will need shelter." He had been keeping the needle pointed east. Allie had seemed surprised he'd recognized the compass, but how did she think his people navigated? Compasses were familiar. But stopping to fill the snowmobile machine with gas every couple of hours was time-consuming to him.

"So, the machine drinks the liquid and burns it in its belly. The heat drives the motor inside it. Is that right?" Kell had cottoned on quickly to the idea of the machine and couldn't wait to take it apart and examine it.

"Exactly." Allie had already explained to him about gasoline and motors. Now they stopped again, filled the tank, stretched their legs, relieved themselves and drank a bit before setting off once more.

They passed through the forest and out onto a flat plain. All around them stretched snowy tundra, but up ahead he saw low hills. They could find shelter there. First they had to cross a large, frozen lake.

"Should we risk going across it, or shall we go around it?" Kell asked.

"It must be frozen solid. Let's cross it. I'm afraid they'll catch up to us." Allie twisted her head to peer behind, and at the same time the snowmobile hit a bump and swerved. Allie's arms slipped from his waist, and he heard a loud thump. In his panic, he forgot to stop the infernal machine. He let go of everything and dove off it, then he leaped toward Allie, lying face down in the snow. She moaned as he reached her, but when he turned her over, he saw that she was unhurt. Relief washed over him, but she cried out in pain the instant he tried to help her get up.

"My shoulder!"

"What is it?" He let go of her arm and stepped back so as not to hurt her more.

She sat up in the snow and held her arm cradled to her chest.

"Is it broken?" he asked, worried.

"I don't think so, just a sprain. But it hurts."

Suddenly he heard a loud cracking sound. Whirling, he turned and saw the machine disappear into a hole in the ice. The supplies! He ran through the snow toward the hole and threw himself flat on his stomach, inching toward the gaping hole. No good. The machine and all that had been on it had disappeared into the icy, dark water. Cursing, he went back to Allie, still lying in the snow.

White-faced, she stared up at him. "What will we do now?"

"If you can walk, we will set out in that direction." He pointed east. "When we get to the nearest hill, I will set up camp and you can rest."

She shook her head. "We don't have time to rest!"

"Don't argue, woman."

They set out at a slow pace. The hills were closer than he had thought, and soon they arrived in a small clearing in a depression surrounded by fir and larch trees. He glanced at the sky. He had an hour, maybe longer. He went to the forest, peeled off chunks of bark, and made crude paddles. Then he scooped snow into them and rapidly patted the snow into a few large bricks. That part was easy, and after stomping down the snow in a circle, he used another piece of bark like a shovel and dug a deep trench inside the circle. Then he dug another foot or so down and again stomped the snow flat.

"Allie, if you stand still you will get cold. Can you go into the woods and try to find dry sticks? The best place to look would be under a fir tree. Bring me the pine cones too."

He watched to make sure she would be all right and heaved a sigh of relief when she moved with no difficulty. Then he got back to work. Quickly, he set the snow bricks down, working in a spiral, and leaning each brick slightly so that the walls sloped inward. He used the bark paddles to make more bricks and piled them at his feet. Soon the walls were waist high.

One more load of snow bricks, and he kneeled in the middle of the circle, placing the bricks carefully until the top met over his head. Only then did he go back to the first bricks and carefully dig down and push them out, making a slightly sunken passage. He crawled out and saw Allie, standing with an armful of branches, her mouth open in a wide O.

"How did you do that?" Allie asked, shaking her head. "That is the most amazing thing I've ever seen."

He shrugged. Everyone who lived in the far north had to know how to do it. He had been trained from childhood to live in the wilderness. Nonetheless, he liked Allie's admiration.

"I'll be right back," he said. The igloo would not keep them warm, and if they had to sit on the ground they would freeze. Already the temperature was dropping alarmingly.

Evening fell. He wished he had his knife, but he broke off branches from fir trees, as many as he could carry, and dragged them into the igloo. Piling these on the ground, he made a sleeping area and left a spot in the middle free for a fire. He found birch trees and peeled off their smooth, soft bark to lay over the fir branches.

He would gather more wood later. Right now he had to get Allie settled. She looked frightened and pale, and she had started shivering.

"Allie, can you crawl through the narrow door inside?" He helped her as much as he could. She had trouble crawling because of her shoulder but never complained.

He thought he would have to spend another hour or so making a fire, but Allie amazed him. She pulled out a small box of tiny twigs from her medicine bag and proceeded to teach him how to make matches work. In no time a small blaze warmed the igloo, the smoke going out of the hole he had left in the roof near the center. Careful to keep the fir branches they sat upon away from the fire, he fashioned a pot from bark and filled it with snow, setting it on a forked branch to heat. He would have to go out two or three times in the night to find firewood, but already the air inside the igloo was starting to get warm.

Once he had gotten everything organized, he turned to Allie. "I have some knowledge of healing. Let me see your arm."

He unfastened her tunic with the little tab she called a zip. Delicately, he extricated her arm from her sleeve and prodded her shoulder. "Does this hurt?"

She nodded. "It hurts horribly."

"The bones are still in place, but it is swelling. Nothing is broken, but your shoulder has been injured and I need to pack snow onto it as soon as possible. Do you have something in your medicine bag to ease the pain?"

Her medicine bag hung over her shoulder and she called it a purse. The matches had been inside it, and she had a tube that shone light too. Very handy, in his opinion. The red stuff she put on her lips, on the other hand, didn't appeal to him at all.

"There should be aspirin in the red box there. Thank goodness that didn't fall into the lake too." She closed her eyes and her face turned a shade paler.

"What is it?"

"I just realized that if I hadn't fallen off, we'd have both crashed into the lake." Tears gathered in her eyes and spilled onto her cheeks.

A jolt of fear shot through him. She spoke the truth. The gods had been watching over them. "Hush, it's all right. Don't cry now. It's all over, and you're fine now."

"Thanks to you."

He opened her medicine bag as he had seen her do before and peered inside. Nothing was familiar to him, and Allie's face got whiter by the minute. He clenched the bag as frustration welled in him. He had never felt so helpless before. "Which thing is aspirin?"

"Give me that bottle," she said, and he did. She opened it and took two pills. "I'll feel better soon," she explained. Then her face brightened. "Here, try this. I think you'll like it." She pulled a flat tablet out of her purse and tore paper from it. A delicious odor filled his nostrils as she handed him a square she'd broken off the tablet. "Go on, eat it."

He had never smelled anything so tempting, but he hesitated.

"Don't you trust me?" She took a small square and nibbled it. "It's very good."

He touched the tip of his tongue to it. Sweet. Rich. Intoxicatingly rich. His mouth literally watered. Sliding it into his mouth, he let the explosion of taste and scent fill his senses. It melted in his mouth, sliding down his throat, rich, sweet, and utterly satisfying. "What is that?" he cried, not wanting it to end. He licked his lips. "Do you have more?"

"It's called chocolate, and I have a little more."

"Chocolate." He sighed happily. "Over two thousand years, but it was worth the wait. Your people have invented a little piece of paradise to eat." He grinned at Allie and kissed the tip of her nose. "Thank you for showing me that I have lots to look forward to discovering in your world. Now, I have to go outside and find some bark to hold the snow. I can use this webbed bandage too."

"What webbed bandage...? Oh, that's my bra." She laughed, but it sounded strained.

"Don't worry. You should try to relax and I'll be right back."

Allie closed her eyes. She had no idea what Kell could do to help her. She couldn't believe her bad luck. She had fallen so hard she'd nearly pulled her shoulder right out of its socket. Thank goodness the bones hadn't broken or the shoulder dislocated, but even so, the pain was just about unbearable. And when they had lost the snowmobile and all their supplies, she'd been sure that they would perish. Only Kell's calm assurance that everything would be all right had saved her from going into hysterics. That, and watching someone actually building an igloo in front of her eyes.

Now she sat on a rather uncomfortable pile of branches, but she was warm, and she was alive, and she still had half a bar of chocolate. If he liked chocolate, just wait until he discovered the joys of hot chocolate and marshmallows.

As soon as the fire showed signs of dying she added twigs and sticks—not too many, just enough to keep a cheerful little fire going. Soon steam rose from the bark container as the snow inside it melted and the water started to boil. The igloo's walls melted a bit and narrow rivulets of water ran down the sides, freezing it and smoothing it. Beneath her, the pine branches gave off a strong, spicy scent.

She drowsed for a while, lulled by the fire's warmth. What seemed like an hour passed, but when she checked her watch, she saw it wasn't more than ten minutes. A little while later, Kell slipped inside the igloo, his arms full of birch tree bark and snow.

He didn't waste time. "Lie down," he ordered. He took her arm and examined it.

"Have you done this before?" she asked.

"As a matter of fact, yes."

He grinned, and she surprised herself by grinning back. For some reason, she trusted him. Besides, what choice did she have?

The pain ebbed as Kell wrapped it tightly with stiff bark, using the extra pair of stockings she'd had in her purse. Carefully, he packed it all with snow and put another layer of bark over it.

"The cold is for the swelling," he said. "You can't put the snow next to your skin, it will burn. The bark will hold the snow and keep your shoulder from swelling too much. We have to keep it cold, I'm afraid. Luckily we have lots of snow."

"Luckily," she whispered, faintness washing over her.

"I'm going back outside. Keep the fire going with this." He pointed to the pile of firewood and she nodded.

For the next few hours, Allie floated between two worlds. She kept drifting in and out of consciousness. Kell came back and, incredibly, he had a fish. *How did he catch a fish?* She had no idea, but she watched, fascinated, while he grilled it. He helped her eat, holding her in his arms. *How can someone be so strong?* He had picked her up out of the snow as if she weighed less than a child, and he'd built an igloo and caught a fish.

He kept adding the snow between the layers of bark so she would heal faster. The pain had almost gone, and only a deep ache remained. She shivered with cold and was thankful for the hot broth Kell had prepared with the rest of the fish and hot water.

Afterward he helped her outside so she could relieve herself. She looked at the night sky, amazed at how close and bright the stars seemed. Then she turned and her breath caught in her throat. In the dark, the igloo glowed like a frosted glass lamp, lit from within by the fire. She forgot the cold and the dark and stared, entranced, at the little igloo. She had never seen anything as lovely in her life. A shiver of pure delight ran over her.

When she crawled back into the igloo, she curled up on the pine branches and tried to get comfortable. Kell cradled her in his arms, and she meant to talk to him. She had so many things to ask him, but her eyelids grew heavy and her head nodded.

"Are you feeling better?"

She looked up, startled. She must have fallen asleep despite the prickly, bumpy branches. Tentatively, she moved her shoulder. No sharp pain appeared. Her head had cleared too, and her panic had worn off. "Yes, thank you."

He sat down next to her with a movement so fluid it took her breath. Truth be told, she couldn't take her eyes off him. She had never seen such a hard-muscled body.

He gave her a wide grin. "What are you staring at?"

Heat flushed her cheeks. "I was staring at you."

He raised an eyebrow. "At me? Does what you see please you?"

He had to be kidding. He was like a Greek statue come to life. "You look like a sculpture I always loved. It's a marble statue of a warrior from Gaul, and there is something about it that reminds me of you."

His eyebrow lifted even higher. "My mother was a Galli, that's what the Romans call the Gauls. My father was a Celt from the Tenes empire. He immigrated south and met my mother. They moved to the island Tu'Og where I was born and lived most of my life."

She wanted to know everything about him. If she could, she would have crawled into his skin and shared all his thoughts and memories. "What year were you born?"

He sat by her side and gently took the layer of bark off her shoulder. "I was born in the year of the wild swan."

That didn't mean anything to her. While he gently manipulated her shoulder, rubbing the stiffness out of it, she thought of how to find out exactly what time period he came from. "Who was emperor of Rome when you were there? Did you hear about Alexander the Great or Jesus? Had Christians arrived in Europe?" All those events had taken place around about the time he had lived. She suddenly found herself wondering if he had seen anyone she'd have heard about.

He held up his hand. "One question at a time, woman! First of all, Rome had no emperor, the kings were banished and it is…sorry…it was a republic." He frowned. "It seems so strange to think we are two thousand years removed from the Rome I knew."

"Did you ever hear of Brennus?"

His face cleared and his eyes shone. "Aye, who hasn't? The Celtic warrior who stormed Rome. My father fought with him. Rome gave Brennus a ransom in gold for not attacking her, and Brennus divided it among his captains. With that money, my father bought a large farm on the island, and thus wooed and won my mother's hand in marriage."

Allie's heart sped up as the implications of what he said sank in. "Did you ever meet Brennus?"

"Aye, he came several times to visit and regaled us with his tales. As a lad, I wanted only one thing—to become a warrior and fight with Brennus."

She could picture him with a shield and a sword, his hair flying in the wind, eyes blazing with fire as he faced his enemy. "Why didn't you?"

"Brennus died, and I did wield a sword, but it was against the invaders from the North." His expression suddenly turned bleak, and she changed the subject.

"Why do you say the year of the swan? What kind of date is that?"

His eyebrows lifted again. "Our tribe has always kept track of time thus. Each year the elders decide what event marked it the most, and they name the year after that. When I was born, ten wild swans came and stayed for a while in our pond."

"Oh."

"I'm just glad I wasn't born the year after. That year the pigs got into the cider bin and ate all the fermented apples."

Allie considered for a minute. "The year of the drunk pig?"

His smile was blinding.

* * * *

"Mr. Steele. We have no time for niceties. Let me fill you in. We're tracking two people, a man and a woman. Here is a photo of the woman, and one of the man."

Steele studied the pictures. He noticed the woman's thick, auburn hair at once, and he wondered if anyone ever saw past her incredible mane. It curled in wild abandon past her shoulders. Whiskey-colored eyes stared at him a bit pugnaciously, and a wide, unsmiling mouth completed the image. Not a raving beauty, but with hair like that, she must have a fiery temperament.

The man's photo intrigued him. He appeared not to notice the camera and looked off into the distance. He had wide, strong shoulders and the tilt of his head suggested a natural arrogance. He had dark-brown eyes — so dark as to be almost impenetrable — and he wore his light-brown hair cut short so that it curled tightly around his head. Steele put the photos down. "What did they do?"

"They've taken something very valuable from this base and we need it back. They left last night on a stolen snowmobile."

"So they have had a twenty-hour head start. Do you have any idea where they are heading? One of the towns here?" He pointed at the map.

"We don't know."

"Where are they from?" Steele knew from experience that people ran toward something familiar.

"The woman is from Montreal. The man is from... Europe."

Steele caught Captain Bide's hesitation but didn't press him. "So they will most likely be heading back to Montreal."

"I have no idea."

"How long did the storm last?"

He paused. "About five hours. It wiped out all the tracks they might have left behind them. We have no indication in what direction they went."

Steele leaned on the table, studying the map. He took a compass and traced a circle, then another. "Let's say they drove for five hours straight and set up camp, waited out the storm then started out again. A snowmobile can go thirty or forty miles an hour. In rough terrain much slower, but it's fairly flat around here, despite the forest. The storm would have slowed them, but not by too much."

"We have a helicopter with everything you need to track them."

"A helicopter. Good. I'll take this map and we'll start with the circles I've drawn. Grid-mark them. Let's go." Steele folded the map and nodded at Captain Bide. "Don't worry, I'll find them."

The captain nodded and shook his hand. Before he left, Steele gazed around the huge hangar. "What is that? It looks like a Viking longhouse."

"It's meant to," said Captain Bide. He didn't offer any more information, and Steele shrugged. He had been hired to find two fugitives, not to ask questions. His curiosity had been sparked, however, and he glanced once more at the antique log house in the middle of the ultra-modern hangar.

"Didn't you have guards for the valuable object?" he asked.

Captain Bide's mouth tightened and he shook his head. "We had a security perimeter, a fence that should have kept anyone out. It never crossed our mind that the thief would operate from the inside."

Steele's interest deepened. He had said thief, not thieves, yet he'd been hired to find two people. And in his experience, inside jobs were the most common when valuable objects were concerned. He said nothing. He simply asked to use the men's room before getting into the helicopter and starting the search. He had been traveling for five hours already and wasn't anxious to sit motionless in a cramped seat again.

When the helicopter lifted off, he had the map on his lap, binoculars around his neck, and an infrared scanner at his disposal in the helicopter. In case they tried to hide beneath the snow, the scanner would pick up their body heat.

The pilot flew the copter above the hangar then spoke to Steele.

"Which way do we go?"

"Toward the nearest town. South."

Chapter Six

The next day, Kell and Allie set out just after dawn. Allie felt much better. Her arm was still sore, but nothing like the sickening pain she had suffered the night before. They trekked over low hills and hadn't gone very far when they heard a voice calling to them. They turned, and Kell saw a dogsled heading toward them.

The first thing Kell noticed was the dogs. They had curly tails and resembled wolves. Tied to a sled, they pulled it like horses. The man standing on the back of the sled wore furs, and for a minute, Kell had the strangest impression he was seeing Vix or Tor. Then reality hit him as if Earth jolted on its axis, and he staggered.

"Are you all right?" Allie asked.

He nodded, unsure of his voice. He had not slept that night, or very little. Worry about Allie and keeping the fire going had kept him awake. He had gone to check his snare, but it had been empty, so they hadn't eaten any breakfast. Allie and he had left the igloo standing. They had planned to walk half the day in one direction, and if they didn't find any settlements, they would turn back and spend the night in the igloo again. But as it transpired, they hadn't walked very long before they had heard barking and the dogs had appeared.

The man drove his dogs up to them and spoke. Kell understood nothing, but Allie did, and soon the man and Allie had come to an understanding.

Allie beamed, her eyes bright with excitement. "I told him we need a place to stay for the night. He knows of a woman who rents a room."

"We need to get a snowmobile," Kell said firmly. He knew the importance of transportation. A man was nothing without his horse, his snowmobile…or his dogs. He noted how the dogs were tied to the man's sleigh, and how easily they pulled it. He tapped Allie's shoulder. "Ask him how fast his dogs go."

"Why?"

"Do they go faster than the snowmobile?"

Allie shook her head. "I don't think so."

"But they would not need to drink gasoline all the time. Do we have far to go?" It seemed to him they had always been stopping to quench the snowmobile's incessant thirst for gasoline.

A pained look crossed her face. "That's true, but I don't know a thing about dogs. I'm sorry."

"We should think about it. I've driven dogsleds before, though none like this one. The ones I knew had only one or two dogs, and they were used to pull a travois." Kell touched her cheek. "Don't look so worried, please."

She had tried to fill him in about the world today as they had walked, and what he would see and hear, and what to expect. He still wondered if he were dreaming sometimes. Mostly, though, he thanked the gods for Allie, and prayed they would never be parted. *But where could we stay? Will we be safe here?*

As if divining his feelings, she took his hand and squeezed it. "This village will be one of the first places they check. We can only stay a little while."

Kell nodded. The man in the furs and the dog sleigh took them to a village, and once again the strangeness of time gone by unnerved him. The houses were made of planks and stood for the most part on stilts. Nothing strange there, but the roofs were made of something he had never seen, and the wooden houses all had such straight walls and clean angles as if they had been made by Romans. The houses all sported coats of bright paint, and he had never imagined such colors for houses—turquoise, yellow and bright red.

71

He shook his head to clear it.

Allie tapped his shoulder. "Are you all right?"

"Aye." He flinched when a giant snowmobile with a roof and windows roared by.

"That's called a pickup truck," Allie said.

He nodded, storing the new words away in his mind. The pickup truck had four large wheels. Pickup trucks were what chariots and horses had become. *Fine, I can handle this.*

Part of him suddenly wanted to learn to drive a pickup truck and go roaring around the streets in it. He could just imagine him and Vix and Tor with one of those machines. They'd have gotten their women back in less than a day. And they would have impressed their tribe to no end if they had shown up in that machine. Even the Romans would have been impressed and it took a great deal to impress a Roman.

That thought fluttered through his mind and left a trail of melancholy in its wake. Vix and Tor had turned to dust... and sometimes his bones seemed to tremble, as if they were about to dry up and blow away on the wind, and all this would have been nothing but a nightmare. Only Allie brought him back to reality and anchored him here.

They pulled the sled up in front of a plank house painted yellow and blue. An old woman opened the door and motioned for them to come inside. Kell helped Allie off the sled and took both backpacks. He nodded politely to the dog master and followed Allie into the modern house, his stomach knotted with nerves.

"Is everything all right?" Allie asked.

He stood in the middle of the kitchen. A squat, cast-iron stove and a basket of firewood reassured him, but some strange cubes with doors, one of which hummed, made him uneasy. He recognized tables and chairs, rugs, and he had known what the sink was, although it was nothing like the Romans' plumbing.

The old woman beckoned them and they followed her down a narrow hallway that gave him claustrophobia. She opened a door and they entered their bedroom.

He noted a wide bed with a blue blanket, a chair, and more strange objects he couldn't find a use for. One was black, square, with a shiny glass front. It had knobs on it, and it faced the bed. There were no oil lamps, but he saw some candles. Desperately he searched for things he knew, and everything he recognized was a small victory for him.

"Will you be all right here?" Allie sounded worried.

He managed to smile and nod and realized how tense his muscles had been. He could barely unclench his jaw to tell Allie he wanted to bathe. "Where are the baths? Are they nearby in the village?"

Allie's face split into a grin. "I have a surprise for you."

"Something I will like?"

"Now, in this time, each dwelling has its own private bath."

That got his attention. Only the great palaces in Rome boasted their own baths. "Is there a hot spring nearby?"

"No, we have heaters that don't take much space." Allie opened a door. "Ta da!"

"Ta da? Is that what you call baths?" He leaned in the doorway, and suddenly all the knots dissolved in his belly. A shiny tub, tiled walls and floor... The world hadn't changed all that much. The Roman baths had survived nearly intact. He shook his head, a huge grin split his face. "What a wonderful ta da."

* * * *

"No one by that description has come here. I'd know, because my brother runs the only bed and breakfast in town." The police officer leaned on his desk, hands clasped, a frown on his face. "Maybe you can tell me why the U.S. military base is sending scouts into Canadian territory? Why didn't they just ask for our help? All they had to do was call."

Steele shrugged. "They didn't even tell me what was missing."

"Damn Yanks. They know we're here to help out, and we've never refused to lend a hand. When the base needed a woodcarver in a rush, we found one and sent him over."

"You did?" Steele hid his interest. "Hmm. Maybe I should talk to him. Where can I find him? Oh, and by the way, are there any more rooms left at your brother's bed and breakfast?"

He took the wood carver's address and thanked the police officer. Outside, the temperature had dropped again and darkness had started to fall. Steele waved to the helicopter pilot, sitting in a bar across the street.

"I'm going to stay here for the night. Tell Captain Bide I'm following some leads. Come pick me up tomorrow at sunrise."

The helicopter pilot nodded and hurried off toward the helipad. He had just enough time to make it back to the base before nightfall.

Steele looked at the address and map the police officer had given him and sighed. All the way across town. He shrugged and stuck out his thumb. A minute later, he had a lift from a granny in a purple snowsuit driving a pickup.

"Where are you headed?" she asked him.

"Jim Leaphorn's place."

"No problem." She didn't bother him with any more questions and he dozed a bit in the too-warm interior of the truck. Until she jammed on the brakes and said, "Here we are!"

He thanked her, slung his backpack on his shoulder, and walked through the gathering darkness to a small log cabin. He knocked. Then, getting no answer, he pushed open the door. Rule Number One in this country, never lock your door. You never know when someone needs to come out of the cold.

Steele made himself useful getting the fire started, then he turned on the lights to let Jim Leaphorn know someone was in his home. Finally he sat down to wait.

He must have fallen asleep, because suddenly something cold was pressed against his shoulder and he heard a deep voice asking, "Who are you, mister?"

His eyes flew open and he thanked his lucky stars he hadn't given in to his first reflex, which had been to leap off the sofa, pull his revolver out of his holster, and start shooting.

The cold thing against his shoulder was a beer, and Jim Leaphorn had a friendly grin on his face. "Startled you, mister? Sorry about that. Not every day I get guests."

Steele put out his hand. "Call me Steele. I'm a tracker, hired by the U.S. Army base up in Night Valley."

"Oh, the secret military base everyone knows about." Jim grinned broadly as he shook Steele's hand. "What are you tracking, Steele?"

"Well, that's where you might be able to help me. See, I wasn't given many details about this case. A man and a woman disappeared, taking something valuable with them. I'm supposed to get it back. But you know the military. They only give you the least amount of information. Sometimes that's not good enough to go on."

"When did this happen?"

"Been more than twenty hours now. I came straight to this village. It's the most obvious place to search. It's the closest, for one, and although they took a snowmobile, a tent and two survival packs, I doubt they want to spend much time in the wilderness."

"Now, why do you say that?" Jim asked.

"Well, the woman is from Montreal. I know absolutely nothing about the man, except that he comes from Europe."

Jim scratched his head. "Well, what do you want from me?"

"You worked there for a while. What exactly did you do? It seemed odd to me that an ultra-modern military base needed a woodcarver."

"Well now, you have a point. Will you stay for dinner?"

Steele blinked. "Sure. Can I help?"

"Well, you did most of the work lighting the fire. I usually just throw whatever I have handy on the grill and put some spuds in the coals."

"Perfect." Steele sat back on the sofa and sipped his beer. "So, tell me. What exactly did you do at the military base?"

Jim's expression was perfectly serious. "I built a Viking longhouse."

* * * *

Steam rose from the water. Allie poked her foot in the air. All wrinkled. Kell, lying in the bath with her, took her foot and nibbled on her toes, his face a study in contentment.

He had been absolutely enthralled with the modern bathroom. From the sink to the bathtub, to the disposable razor and shaving cream, he'd had a blast. There was shaving cream all over. He hadn't been able to stop squirting it out of the can. Then he had found the radio, and after he'd understood how it worked, he had to try all the stations sixty times. He had settled on country-western, and every once in a while he'd pick up a refrain and sing it.

Allie was discovering new things about him every minute. For one thing, he had an uncanny sense of mimicry and could imitate motions and sounds perfectly. He would watch her do something, his attention fixed on her like a laser beam, then he would do what she'd done without fault. The same applied to language. When he heard something, he would parrot it. Music was just one facet. He was rapidly picking up words for everything, and he never seemed to forget one. He loved to imitate and listened to everything, including commercials.

"There's a brand-new car in your future," he sang. "What does it mean, Allie?"

She explained, and he nearly choked laughing. Then he sang the refrain from the commercial again, translating it into Roman and Celt, never missing a beat.

"Where did you learn the languages you speak?" she asked.

"I learned Latin from a tutor and Celt from my father. The druids taught us the language of the Galli, but they would not write anything down. To them it was a sacrilege. We learned to listen," he explained with a shrug. "So I picked up Pict, Copt and a few other languages. How are your children taught?"

"In schools." He tickled her toes then sucked on them.

His tongue was devilish, and she sighed, leaning back in the water. He slid his hand up her calf and to her thigh.

"Such soft skin, so smooth." He chuckled and nipped her instep. "Even your feet are soft and smooth. So tell me, Allie. Do you think we could get a dogsled? We don't have to feed the dogs gasoline, and we can travel more lightly without those big heavy cans."

She didn't want to talk. She wanted him to touch her some more, so she shifted a bit in the water, opening her legs. His legs, beneath her, tensed then relaxed. A sly grin lit his face, and he placed his hand firmly on the small of her back. Strong fingers began to massage her, rubbing and circling the two dimples on either side of her backbone. The massage began to tingle and he very slowly drew his finger down her spine and into the crack of her buttocks.

He stopped there, lightly resting his finger on her anus. Her pussy contracted as if he had just touched her clit. She gave a little gasp. His grin grew even wider.

Wet, his hair curled into tight ringlets, lifting off his temples and the back of his neck. He'd shaved, and now she could clearly see the cleft in his chin and the square jaw that made him seem rugged. But his high cheekbones and almond-shaped, bright-with-mischief eyes gave him an almost puckish look. Added to the effect were a devastating grin and the strongest muscles she had ever seen. No wonder her whole body quivered when he was near. And when he touched her…

"Oh, my God," she whispered as his finger drew slow

circles around the sensitive skin of her anus. Each time he prodded her gently, her cunt answered with a surge of heat and desire.

"Which god do you invoke?" he asked, parting her legs farther and using his other hand to stroke her cleft, starting at her clit and sliding back toward her vagina.

"I only have one," she managed to gasp as he fingered her clit and at the same time, inserted his fingertip into her ass.

"Just one? How boring. What do you call him?"

"Lord!" Allie gasped as his finger prodded her.

"We call this a puckered rosebud." He wiggled his finger in her ass.

Sharp spasms ran from her belly to her thighs, and Allie couldn't suppress a low moan.

"It is pleasing to a woman to have her husband service her in this way," he murmured, kneeling over her.

She floated in the warm water, her head on the edge, holding on for dear life to the sides, while Kell slid his finger into her ass and flicked at her clit with his other hand.

Then he leaned down, took one of her nipples in his mouth, and sucked on it, pulling it with his lips and nibbling the tip gently with his teeth.

He put a finger into her cunt too, slippery even in the bath water, and thrust. Fullness overwhelmed her. Her pussy ached, little tremors making it clench in time to her pounding heart. Her ass tingled, the finger prodding nerve endings she never knew she had…and sending such a strong, throbbing heat through her body she could hardly breathe. And his mouth on her breast… *Oh, Lord. Can I come this quickly?*

Her chest grew tighter and she had to gasp for breath. All she could think of was the finger thrusting hard into her cunt and the finger in her ass, both moving in and out, in and out, making a wicked heat that grew like an out-of-control blaze. The heat washed over her, submerged her, lifted her so high she nearly screamed. Then she shattered, her cunt and ass contracting madly, clamping down on his fingers as she wrapped her legs around him. She shivered into a million pieces, a tingling rush of pleasure exploding inside her. She melted, dissolving into the tub, losing her legs, her arms, herself in the violent paroxysms of lust.

If he hadn't held her, she would have slid underwater. But he cradled her in his strong, strong arms. He crooned into her ear, soft sounds that caught her and wrapped her in warmth. He kept his arms around her while her body arched against him and little cries burst from her throat. She couldn't stop coming, and she didn't want to. Kell was there. He held her, and was strong enough to keep her safe.

When the tremors faded, and her heartbeat slowed, she opened her eyes. Kell's face was close to hers, his eyes and lips tender. He bent and kissed her, and no one had ever kissed her so gently and so forcefully at the same time. As his lips pressed to hers, her cunt gave another massive twinge and a rush of liquid heat burst from her.

He gently thrust his finger into her, easing the tension that still coiled within her.

Finally, she could draw a deep breath and she uttered an incredulous laugh. "I never believed I could come so hard."

Kell cocked his eyebrow and gave her a wide smile. "Then I will have the pleasure of teaching you just how hard you can come." He shifted and his hard-on pressed against her buttocks. "And you will see how hard I can come."

He stepped out of the tub, his cock erect, and stretched, his muscles rippling beneath his skin. Mutely, Allie held up her arm. She couldn't move. It was as if her muscles had dissolved in the bath. Seizing her arms, he pulled her to her feet.

"There are towels on the heater." Allie pointed in their direction.

She had hardly gotten the words out of her mouth when she found herself wrapped up in a thick towel and carried to the bed. Dumped among the covers, she didn't have time to take a breath before Kell had plunged his head between her legs and was happily lapping at her cunt.

"Give me a man with an agile tongue, and I won't need rubies or gold." Kell raised his head and winked at her. "That's what I always heard from the wise-woman of our village." He lowered his head and his tongue parted her swollen flesh and swiped upward, flicking over her clit like velvet lightning.

Allie didn't know what to reply to that. Besides, the wise woman obviously knew what was best — give her a choice between rubies and a man with an agile tongue and she'd... Oh! Her back arched of its own violation and her knees parted wide. She grabbed at his head, pressing it closer to her, as wave after wave of surging contractions seemed to twist her insides out.

With a groan, Kell raised himself over her then plunged his cock straight into her sex. Her sheath grabbed his cock tightly, and Allie threw her head back and cried out as the tip slid into her, right to her cervix. He thrust, filling her completely, then stayed perfectly still.

Each muscle quivered, and a drop of water trickled down his temple and cheek. He held his breath, concentrating on his cock buried in Allie's body, letting his sex join them as one being. When she breathed, he breathed, and when her heart beat, so did his. Her legs trembled, and an answering quiver ran up his thighs and spine. Her pulse beat in her womb, throbbing in the tip of his cock, and surging backward down his cock to his balls and belly.

She let out a low moan, and a flutter of clutching pulsations massaged his cock. Her head swung back and forth, her eyes closed, her mouth open as little cries left her throat. A tingle grew in his balls and his cock started to throb. He could no longer hold back. With a mighty roar, he pounded his hips into hers, his balls slapping against her buttocks, his cock squeezed tight in a hot, wet sheath.

Her nipples hardened brushing against his chest, and he thrust again and again, letting her cunt milk his seed from his cock and surging from his body in a long, almost painful outpouring.

Exhausted, drained, he dropped to her side, holding her in his arms and burying his face in the crook of her neck. Warmth stole over him, and contentment as he'd never known. Had his fate ever been to sleep two thousand years to find the woman of his life? That notion claimed him even as sleep pulled his eyelids down and quieted his breathing.

I'm home at last, he thought before he fell asleep. *I have come to this time, and here I will stay, as long as Allie is by my side.*

* * * *

Kell's eyes fluttered open. Allie sat in the bed next to him, her attention fixed on something behind his shoulder. He turned his head and nearly fell off the bed.

"Argh!" he cried, a stab of panic jerking him upright. Inside the black box, a man's head spoke. Heart pounding, he grabbed Allie's arm. "What happened to him? What sorcery keeps him alive?"

Allie shook her head. "Not sorcery, technology. The same technology that sends the music to the radio box sends images to this box. It's a television. This is the weather station."

Kell shuddered. The man had been cut off at the torso, and he sat in the box and spoke earnestly… The image blinked and changed and suddenly he stared at a bright, shiny pickup truck barreling straight toward them.

With a hoarse cry, he flung himself on Allie and pushed her off the bed. "Watch out!" he yelled.

She landed with a cry and a thump, and instantly someone pounded on their door and yelled something unintelligible.

"I'm sorry," Kell said as the door opened and the old lady peered in worriedly.

She said something to Allie who must have reassured her, because the woman shrugged and closed the door again. Kell glanced at the infernal box, where the pickup had disappeared, leaving its place for a singing fish.

He started to shake. He couldn't help it. A fish wearing a hat was singing. He backed up until he hit the wall, his eyes fastened to the terrifying sight. A crab and another fish joined the first fish, and they all sang and danced.

"Am I having a nightmare?" he said when he could get his voice back.

Allie sat up and took his face in her hands. "It can't hurt you," she whispered, her voice soft. "I would never put you in danger. Do you believe me?"

He tore his eyes from the singing fish and nodded. "Yes." He couldn't stop shaking, though.

Allie wrapped her arms around him, rocking him gently. She whispered in his ear. "The television is our entertainment, and it gives us information. The biggest difference between your world and ours is communication. We send sound and images through the air and they are captured in these boxes. When something happens it shows up on television or we hear about it on the radio."

Kell considered that, his forehead resting on her shoulder. "So if the barbarians invade Rome, it would be on this television box? Everyone all over the world would know?"

"Yes. They would know the same day it happened."

Kell risked a glance at the television box. To his relief, the fish had vanished and now a woman washed a floor with a mop. He pointed at the woman and frowned. "Don't you feed your slaves?"

Allie blinked and looked over his shoulder. "That's not a slave, we don't have slaves. And what do you mean about not feeding her?"

"She's so thin, no muscle tone at all, and underfed. It's terrible!" He made a face and caught sight of Allie's expression. "What is it?"

"Nothing. Oh, Kell, nothing at all." Her face broke into a huge grin and she gave him an enormous hug. "I think I love you, and I don't know how I'm going to be able to leave you," she whispered.

He raised his eyebrow. "Why would you leave me? I

know I love you, Allie. I knew it the moment I saw you."
She opened her mouth to speak but he put his hand on her
lips. "No, don't speak. I don't want you to argue with me,
and I can see you are about to argue. We will talk about
leaving or not leaving another time. Can you make the
images stop? I've had enough for one day."

She took a deep breath and nodded. "I'm sorry. I should
have warned you, but I didn't want to wake you." She
pushed a small button and the television turned all black
again. But Kell didn't feel better until he had draped at
towel over it, and even then he had the impression eyes
peeped out from it and watched him.

* * * *

"A Viking longhouse." Steele propped his chin on his
hands and gazed at the fire. "What else can you tell me?"

"It was pretty tense working there. A huge part of the
hangar had been sectioned off, and armed guards patrolled
morning, noon and night."

The mystery deepened. According to Captain Bide, there
hadn't been any guards because they couldn't imagine
anyone stealing the object. So what had happened? The
longhouse finished, the guards then left. A linguist comes,
and that night she and another man disappear. "What was
being guarded?"

"I'm not sure." Jim shook his head, prodding the steaks
sizzling on the grill.

The scent of baking potatoes started to fill the room. Steele
always likened the smell of baked potatoes to chocolate,
and his mouth watered.

"Surely you have an idea. How long did you work there?"

"Long enough to draw some pretty crazy conclusions."

"I like crazy conclusions." Steele grinned, taking a plate
and digging the foil-wrapped potatoes from the ashes.

"What do you think about a longhouse built right down
to the slightest detail to be authentic?"

"Authentic?"

"Yeah, let's say late Iron Age. There were carvings they asked me to do in the wooden beams that I recognized from history classes at the university. They were Celtic. They had furs and pottery, a central fireplace and oil lamps. Everything had to be perfect. They fired one guy who brought in a pronghorn trophy one day. Their reason was this — pronghorns didn't exist in Europe."

"Bad luck for him," said Steele. He tore the foil off the potatoes and sighed in contentment. "Baked potatoes are the best..." He broke off and looked at Jim. "Wait a minute, say that again."

"What?"

"Pronghorns don't exist in Europe. They made an Iron Age longhouse that had to be set in Europe, and nowhere else." Steele put down his plate and started to pace. "A longhouse from Europe. Guards that disappear when the longhouse is completed. A linguist. Why a linguist? That bothers me the most." He shook his head. "What would a linguist be needed for? I can understand a stonemason, a woodcarver, a specialist in skins and trophies... All that can be explained by the completed longhouse. Everyone but a linguist."

Jim put the steaks on their plates and sat back, a bemused expression on his face. "Unless they somehow had an Iron Age man they needed to talk to."

A shiver ran down Steele's spine. "A secret military base. A bunch of scientists and soldiers." He stopped pacing and faced Jim. Urgently he asked, "What would you do if you had a man from the past? A man frozen for thousands of years. He wakes up. What do you need?"

"You need to wake him up slowly and not frighten him. It wouldn't do any good to have him wake up and die of a heart attack, and you need someone to tell him to relax and cooperate." Jim chuckled then grew solemn. He peered closely at Steele. "You're not serious. Wait a minute. Hell, you are serious!"

"It all fits together. The man from Europe was the valuable object that's missing, only he wasn't stolen, he ran away. Or the woman stole him. What did Captain Bide say? Thief, not thieves. The thief was the woman, and the stolen object was a man from the past." Steele thought of the photo he had been shown of the man's face. He hadn't been looking at the camera, he had been unaware his photo was being taken. He had an air of being strong and capable.

"That creates more questions than it answers," said Jim, putting butter on his steaming potato. "Why did she steal him? Or did they run away together? Why didn't Captain Bide level with you? What were they doing with a Celtic guy, anyway?"

Steele rubbed his hand over his face. "I don't know. Another possibility is that the whole thing is a hoax. Or a misunderstanding. But let's run with the idea that there really was someone from a bygone era, and the woman somehow managed to escape with him."

"You have to find out why the man agreed to run away with the woman." Jim nodded. "If he left of his own free will, then that means they were running away from something. Unless the woman believes she can somehow cash in on kidnapping a man from the past. What do you think?"

"I have to get back to the base as soon as possible. Is there a helicopter that can fly me there tonight?"

"No, sorry, you're stuck here. Why? What's the hurry?"

"If the man came from the Iron Age, the last place he'd go would be a town or city. He'd head inland...or toward the coast. A small village would be more familiar to him. He wouldn't mind spending weeks in the wilderness. With just a branch and a stone he could get food, build a fire, and survive. These people knew how to survive in extreme conditions." Steele frowned at his plate. "I went in the wrong direction. Now I have to start all over."

Damn. Why hadn't Captain Bide told him in the first place? What else was he hiding?

Chapter Seven

Allie gave in to the dogsled idea. Kell's arguments were persuasive. The dogs wouldn't need gas, and they could take enough dog food with them to last a week or more, whereas the snowmobile needed gas more often. Allie wrote a check for a dog team and sled, an ultra-modern tent, plus a rifle and ammunition. Thank goodness her purse always stayed on her shoulder.

They hadn't spoken again about love or leaving each other. Allie was afraid to bring up the subject. Afraid Kell had just said that out of fear, afraid that he would decide he'd rather be alone...or with someone else. She had seen him staring at the women in the village as they'd walked down the streets. No, she shook her head sharply. He stared at everyone, not just women. He hadn't seemed the least bit interested in the pretty woman who'd sold them the rifle and ammunition. She had tried to flirt with Kell in a friendly fashion, but Kell hadn't responded, and she'd given up with a curious glance in Allie's direction.

Allie sighed and supposed she would get used to it someday—being stared at because she was the one with Kell, that was. Kell's incredible physique and feline grace made her feel even plainer and more awkward, but to be honest, his eyes only sparkled when he looked at her. It mystified her, and at the same time she wondered how long it would last.

His curiosity knew no bounds. He had insisted on taking a ride in a pickup truck, and when they'd gone to the small port to see the boats, he had been thrilled with the motors. He had been disappointed that the spring ice prevented any boats from leaving the port. He'd wanted to see how fast they went. What was it with men and speed?

Kell, with Allie as translator, spoke to the dog master and they learned how to care for and harness the dogs. Then they had gone to the shooting range. Kell proved to be a natural with a rifle, which didn't surprise Allie. "I think it's in the genes. Little boys take a stick as soon as they're able to pick it up and try to whack something with it, and then they aim and shout 'bang, bang!'"

"What did you say?" Kell peered into the scope and sighted the target. He pressed the trigger and a hole appeared right next to the bullseye. His glance at her was pure satisfaction.

"Good shot!"

"I know." Kell flashed her a wide grin.

"My, aren't you modest."

His eyebrow rose. "No one has ever called me that before."

"I can't understand why." Allie kept her face straight and pointed at the target. "It's a tiny bit to the left."

"Yes, well, I have to adjust the…scope. My English is improving, isn't it?"

"Amazing. But I don't want to praise you too much or you'll get a big head."

"A big head? You mean conceited? Me?"

"I think you've had enough rifle practice today. Let's go get the dogs and head out. I'm worried that they'll find us here."

The noon siren had just sounded from the village. The morning had been busy but now everything had been settled.

Kell patted her arm. "All right. I can sense your disquiet. The weather is going to change again, so perhaps we should leave and get away from the village before dark." He slung the rifle over his shoulder and strode away, his boots crunching the snow.

"How do you know the weather will change?" She hurried to catch up to him.

He glanced down at her and shrugged. "Small signs like the shift in the wind direction, the cloud formation, and the way my scalp prickles. Our druid taught us how to watch for these things. Don't your teachers tell you this?"

"Um, no. We have the weather station."

"The place where the man had his body cut off?"

Allie blinked then remembered his fright when he had seen the television. "Not exactly." She had to describe the weather station to him as they walked through the village. Allie noticed it seemed quiet, but Kell stopped and gazed around.

"Where is everyone?" he asked.

"Maybe they're at work," Allie said, explaining that most people worked during the day.

They arrived at the yard where their sled waited, loaded and ready to go. The dogs waited too, picketed to stakes on short ropes, their expressions eager. There was only one sad face in the yard. The dog trader's son sat on the top of the porch steps, his face glum.

"Ask the boy why he is so sad." Kell pointed at the child.

She shrugged and approached him. He was about nine or ten, with a round face and a snub nose already pink from the cold. "What's the matter?"

He sighed. "My little brother is missing. My dad and mom are out looking for him, and I'm supposed to stay here in case he comes back."

Allie gasped and translated for Kell.

"So that's why it is so quiet here. Everyone is out searching for the little boy. Which way did he go?" Kell glanced around, frowning. "We are close to the woods here, but maybe he took the street into town."

The boy pointed toward the forest. "We think he went there."

Kell said, "Ask him to show me exactly where he last saw his brother."

The boy hopped off the steps and pointed to a spot in front of his parents' snowmobile. "He was right over here."

Kell got to his hands and knees and examined the ground. Then he stood and, still looking at the ground, started off toward the woods. Before he got there, he stopped and kneeled in the snow, brushing it a bit and frowning. "He didn't go into the forest. He went this way."

The boy raised his eyebrows. "That goes back toward the village."

"Does he know anyone there?" Allie asked.

The boy grimaced. "Everyone in the village, and everyone knows he's missing. If he went to someone's house, we would have heard about it by now."

Kell listened to Allie's translation and nodded. "I will follow his tracks. Isn't there a tracker here?"

Allie shook her head. "They might track bear and caribou, not little boys."

Kell followed the boy's trail and found him under a porch in the village, asleep, curled up with two dogs. He called to Allie and she crawled under the porch and woke up the little boy. By the time they got back to the dog trader's house, everyone had gathered in the yard.

The boy's brother had called them with a talking box. Allie explained that it was a telephone and was used for communication. To Kell, it seemed like talking to spirits. He cringed when they held the box to their ears and spoke into thin air. But everyone was relieved and joyful. Everyone shook his hand, the women hugged him, and some cried.

They seemed to be making a fuss about nothing, but Allie explained that another child had gone missing last year and had been killed by a wild animal. This little boy's family had been frantic with worry.

The man insisted on giving Kell a gift, and he pressed some paper into his hand. Kell was mystified until Allie explained that it was money. He thanked the man, using the new words he had learned, then accepted his help to get the sled ready. He had caught Allie's mood and knew she wanted to be off. He would have liked to stay in the village longer. The people seemed kind and he had enjoyed everything...except the television box. If he got a dwelling, he wouldn't put the box in the bedroom because it distracted him.

Allie watched Kell as he harnessed the dogs, calling each one by name and keeping them in order. As with everything, he had only needed to be shown once, and he already acted as if he had been a dogsled driver all his life.

"Allie, you sit here under the furs so you won't be cold. I will stay behind and be the mush." He seemed to love scattering English and slang words in his sentences, but sometimes he got words slightly wrong.

"It's musher. Are you sure I won't be too heavy?"

He tilted his head, considering, then shook it. "No. Now, sit." He pointed to the sled with his whip.

"Yes, master," she said, only half-joking. When he gave an order, she knew he expected to be obeyed instantly.

The dogs knew this too and reacted to his natural authority with a slavish obedience. They came in all shapes, sizes and colors, but all were husky-types, and they whined in anticipation. They seemed to love pulling the sled, and when Kell gave the word, they shot off so fast Allie had to grab the sides of the sled.

"Wow!" she cried.

Kell laughed in sheer delight and the sound lifted Allie's heart. She loved his laugh, so open and so completely sincere. He trotted after the sled, standing on the runners in the back when the dogs ran, walking next to the sled as soon as they slowed. Within no time the village disappeared from sight, and they found themselves in the vast wilderness.

Allie had a map of the area with all the paths and tracks clearly marked. The dogsled driver had given it to them, and she pointed out the way to go. Most of the tracks had been well traveled and so they made good time. Soon, however, snow began to fall and their pace slowed.

"You were right. It's snowing now." She peered into the

gathering darkness. "Is it a storm?"

"Maybe." He didn't seem concerned.

"Do you think we should start finding shelter?"

"I've been looking. There is a ridge not far. It will block the wind. We'll cross it and camp on the other side."

Only then did Allie notice the direction the wind blew, and the high, sharp ridge he spoke of. She shivered despite the furs. Alone, she would have no chance in the wilderness. Kell seemed as at home here as in an apartment. No, he would surely be less at home in an apartment. Here, he was in his element.

They crossed the ridge and sure enough, the wind didn't blow as hard. Kell unhitched the dogs and made sure they were securely picketed, then got the tent set up. The snow came down faster now, but the dogs needed food and water before they could curl up and sleep out the storm. Kell took care of everything with an economy of movement that was pure poetry to watch. She wanted to help, even just to give the dogs their rations, but Kell pointed to the tent. "Inside. Make dinner for us... Please," he added, giving her a charming grin.

When he came back in his face seemed pale with fatigue.

She didn't want to seem worried about him, so she said, "Are you sure the dogs will be all right?"

He undressed, hanging up his parka, and stretched his hands toward the camp stove, sighing contentedly. "They have always slept outdoors and they will be fine."

"Kell..." She hesitated. "I'm not sure how we're going to get to Iceland. We have to find a boat, and to do that we have to find a seaport. There are a few, but they will be far bigger than the cities you are used to."

"I've been to Rome, what can be bigger?"

"Our cities are much bigger than Rome."

"Like Thebes or Babylon, then?"

She hesitated. "Do you trust me?"

He yawned and took her hands in his. "Allie, as the god Lugh brings light to the world, so I swear that I trust you."

"Our cities will terrify you, but if you stay close to me, nothing will hurt you. The noise will be unbearable, but don't worry about it, you'll adapt. That's what I'm trying to say. I have the utmost confidence that you will adapt."

"Thank you, Allie," he said gravely. Then he pulled her to him and wrapped his arms around her, holding her to his chest, his chin resting on the top of her head.

She snuggled into his arms. She had always wanted a man who could take care of her, someone who would protect her and make her feel secure. Kell didn't know anything about this world, and he was unprepared to face it. Nonetheless, the way he had accepted everything told her that he could overcome whatever he had to in order to adjust. He might not ever truly fit in, or feel right in this time. But she had confidence in his abilities. And when he held her in his arms, she knew nothing could happen to her. Nothing.

* * * *

"Why didn't you tell me the truth?" Steele leaned back in his chair and fought the urge to put his foot on Captain Bide's impeccably ordered desk.

"We have no intention of letting our discovery become common knowledge. Whatever conclusions you've reached, there is no way to prove anything and we'll never corroborate any story you'd want to tell."

"I didn't plan on telling stories. If you hired me, it's because you know all about me, and I didn't get my reputation by blabbing."

"Exactly." Captain Bide smiled. The smile didn't reach his eyes. "The woman is highly expendable. The man is more valuable, and we'd much prefer to have him captured alive."

Steele shifted in his chair, suddenly uncomfortable. Something about Captain Bide made him uneasy. He didn't let anything show, however, and just nodded.

Captain Bide put his fingertips together and looked at

Steele over them. Finally, he shrugged. "How would you like to triple the amount you're getting?"

"Triple?" That caught him off-guard.

"All you have to do is make sure the woman never tells anyone about our...project."

The prickle of disquiet grew, but Steele kept his expression bland. "Why don't you put the new amount in my contract, and I'll see what I can do."

"It's always a pleasure working with a professional." Bide shook Steele's hand, a smirk on his face.

Steele just nodded curtly and left the small office. He managed not to wipe his hand on his pants until he reached his room. There, he sat and mulled over everything he had learned.

* * * *

Kell woke at dawn. The sky had just taken on a pink tinge, and the air had that clear, rock crystal appearance that he loved. After leaving the tent to write his name in the snow, he found a clean drift and rolled in it, the icy snow burning his skin, then he washed up a bit with a cloth he had taken from the tent. He used a green twig to clean his teeth, and at that moment, facing nothing but endless pine forest and snow, he could believe he was still back in his time.

Naked, he stood in the snow until his feet began to ache with the cold. Only then did he turn around and slowly lift his gaze to the tent. As always, a shock ran through him at the wrongness of it. Nothing natural emanated from the tent. Nothing seemed earthy or part of nature. Only one thing good about that tent — Allie. He slipped inside and stared at her as she lay peacefully sleeping. Too peacefully. He grinned.

Then her eyes flickered open. She stared up at him, and it pleased him to note the admiration he saw there. His cock, stiff and engorged, ached with desire and he stroked it, letting her see his need for her. As he stroked himself, he could see her pupils getting darker, and her eyes, usually a limpid, light brown, grew cloudy. She swallowed hard, a flush appearing on her cheeks.

Slowly, he kneeled next to Allie and nuzzled her neck, licking the melting snow off her skin. Her hair brushed his cheeks and her scent, light and flowery, tickled his nose. He slid his hand down into the sleeping bag and cupped her breast, rubbing her nipple gently with his thumb.

Nipples had been made to be sucked. He pushed the sleeping bag down to her waist and lowered his mouth to her hard nipple. He loved when she writhed and moaned, and her nipple hardened even more as he licked it.

Growling softly, he raked his hands down her sides. "I want you," he said hoarsely,

Her breathing had gotten harsh and her eyes had turned the color of that food he loved above all others…chocolate. No, there was something he loved even more—the taste of Allie. He nibbled a line of kisses down the inside of her thigh and she gave a little cry.

His cock jumped at her soft cry, and a drop of his seed pearled on the tip. His balls tightened almost painfully. "Not yet," he snarled at his quivering shaft. The idea of slipping it into her tight sheath and thrusting to the hilt sent another stab of desire through him, but he was made of sterner stuff than that. Pushing her knees apart, he admired her swollen pussy gleaming in its setting of short, auburn curls. Pale pink outer lips begged to be stroked, and he did, first with his finger then with his tongue.

Salty, musky juice made his cock stiffen further, and when he tongued her slit and dived into it, he nearly lost control of his raging hard-on. Allie raised her hips, pressing herself closer. He flicked his tongue against her clit and chuckled when she uttered a long, drawn-out gasp.

His chuckle turned into a groan and the scent and taste of her arousal seemed to penetrate his veins and heat his entire body with a single craving to shoot his seed as hard as he could into the depths of her body. Rising onto his forearms, he arched his back and placed the tip of his cock just in the entrance of her passage...and he stayed perfectly still. She tried to lift her hips to impale herself on him, but he took her shoulders in his hands and pressed down. "Don't move," he ordered, his voice rough with desire.

He could sense her need, rising and cresting like a wave. When she threw back her head and uttered a ragged cry, he thrust down, putting all his weight into it, feeling her body open and welcome him at the same time her hunger reached its peak and burst. Her cunt milked his cock, the hard ring of muscle at the entrance pulsing in time to her heartbeat. He plunged to the root of his cock then held himself still to enjoy the contractions shaking her. Shivers of sheer delight ran down his spine and he could hold off no longer. His hips thrust of their own accord, his cock slipping in and out of her wetness, churning into her until all he saw were stars and his breath came in short gasps.

Heat slammed through him, rising from his loins to the top of his skull. Then he had the impression that his heart had stopped as a spring seemed to uncoil inside him. His cock jerked while stream after stream of seed shot from it, and he collapsed onto Allie, holding her, he eruption shaking him. He cried out then, the sound ripped from his throat, and afterward the silence was like that after a storm. The tent shivered with it.

"Allie," he murmured, burying his face in the crook of her neck.

She wrapped her arms around him and fell asleep again, her mouth soft, her face peaceful.

He was tempted to sleep too, but instead, he eased out of the sleeping sack so as not to wake Allie, and slid into his clothes. He pulled on his boots, marveling for the hundredth time at how clothes had changed. Heavy, hand-stitched skins had given way to light silken garments that weighed hardly anything and kept his skin warm and dry.

He picked up his gun then shook his head and set it down. They had enough food, he didn't need to hunt. Outside, the dogs had woken and they stood and shook the snow off their backs. They wagged their tails, happy to see him, and he set them free, watching as they rushed around sniffing, playing and mock-fighting.

Whistling, he slapped his thigh and the dogs bounded after him. He walked through the forest for an hour, keeping an eye on the dogs, but they didn't stray far. A soft breeze stirred the tree branches, and he stood still, feeling the warmth of spring starting to creep into the air. Spring. He tilted his head back, baring his throat. In a few weeks he should be celebrating the spring solstice. This year he would celebrate with Allie.

He paused, looking down at the valley behind him. Was he attaching too much importance to things from the past? Did anyone still celebrate the solstices? Allie had mentioned one god. What had happened to the others? Had they fought, and only the strongest survived? What did it even matter?

Too many questions jumbled in his head and he had no answers. Time would tell him what he had to know and time… A noise startled him and he whirled around. It sounded like a pickup truck, only louder. It got louder and prickles of fear ran up his spine. The dogs didn't seem concerned, so it must be something they had heard before. He looked around, but the sound grew even louder and came from…above?

Heart thudding, he looked upward. In the distance, he saw something like a huge wasp. It approached, and he realized that it must be huge enough to carry humans. Fear iced his blood, but he had never been paralyzed by fear. He had faced enemies, and this was simply a machine, a pickup truck that flew. He forced his legs to move, to carry him toward the tent and Allie, and toward the flying wasp machine that approached the valley with what seemed like sinister intent.

Allie finished packing. Kell and the dogs had gone for

a walk. She'd seen their tracks in the fresh snow. She had made a Thermos of coffee and some sandwiches. Kell had become obsessed with coffee, chocolate and peanut butter and jelly sandwiches. He had a sweet tooth and had adored everything he had tried so far. And she adored Kell.

She sighed as she put away the sleeping bags. Warm taffy described how her body felt. Kell knew how to push her buttons, that was for sure. She was dejected at the thought. She couldn't tie him down. She had to let him go. Women always tied down men. If she really loved him, she would set him free.

Packing the camp stove away, she wondered if she confused men with wild animals. But her father had left her mother when she had been just a child, and her mother's boyfriends had all complained her mother had smothered them, leaving one after the other. Allie had sworn she'd never stifle anyone. And she never had.

She stared at a spot on the floor and frowned. Actually, she had never gotten close enough to anyone to stifle him. She had never fallen in love with a man. The realization stunned her for a second. Love. She had gotten so good at keeping it at arm's length. Her heart had a wall around it ten feet thick and made of ice. A shiver ran through her. If the wall melted, her heart would be exposed, raw, easy to break.

She shook her head sharply. No, best not to fall in love, especially not with someone as freedom-loving as Kell. He would not take to being smothered by anyone. Anyway, he had to grow tired of her soon enough, she supposed. The idea depressed her, so she turned back to the packing. The sound of a helicopter approaching drove away all those thoughts.

Hurriedly, she took the backpacks out of the tent, unhooked the stove, and started to take down the tent. The chopper circled, and to her horror, started to descend. Oh, God, they'd found her. Thank goodness Kell had gone. If only she had stayed hidden. She hesitated then stowed the tent onto the sled. *Act natural*, she said to herself. If she ran and hid in the trees, the pilot would be suspicious. Smiling brightly, she waved toward the helicopter.

Steele held the binoculars to his eyes and scanned the trees. After talking to Captain Bide and convincing the man to level with him, he was confident he would find the couple in a matter of days, if not hours. He had plotted another chart, this one heading northeast, toward the coast. There he'd found a few likely places. This village was first on his list. He motioned to the helicopter pilot to circle over a ridge and approach from the south. If the couple had been here, he'd find out soon enough.

He glanced again out of the window, and that's when Lady Luck smiled at him. A twinkle in the distance caught his eye. Through the binoculars, the twinkle became the sparkle of light on a Mylar tent. Adjusting the image, he saw a dogsled parked next to the tent.

As he watched, someone ducked out of the door of the tent and started to take it down. The person looked toward him, and he saw it was a woman. A small, compact woman with dark red hair. From this distance he couldn't see her features, but he grinned in satisfaction.

"Bingo," he murmured.

He had found them. But the woman didn't act panic-stricken. Instead she waved in a friendly fashion.

Had he been wrong? Sudden doubt assailed him. He scanned the area, looking for the man. Nothing. He was too far away to see any tracks.

Could she be a villager out on a camping trip? Where were her dogs? How many red-haired women were in the area? He must have found the people he sought.

He motioned to the pilot. "Set down as close as you can to that ridge."

The pilot nodded. "No problem. There's a flat field nearby."

Steele kept an eye on the woman while the helicopter

descended. She didn't seem worried. She loaded the sled, packing everything away with practiced ease. His doubts continued to grow, but it would only take a few minutes to verify her identity.

Snow flew in a cloud when the helicopter landed. Steele put down the binoculars and reached for his seatbelt when an ominous cracking sounded.

"Shit!" The pilot slammed the lever forward, seeking to regain altitude. But the field had turned out to be a small pond covered with snow, and the helicopter's weight broke the ice, plunging it sideways.

For Steele, it seemed everything went in slow motion. The rotor blade hit the ground and shattered. Ice and water sprayed in a brown and white geyser, and sparks and smoke suddenly erupted from the engine. His seat belt bit into his flesh, his head snapped backward, and something hit him hard on the side.

No pain, no fear...only the impression of being a rat shaken by a terrier, then darkness.

Kell slipped through the trees, keeping out of sight of the flying machine. It approached the tent then started to land just behind the ridge. But something went wrong. Instead of settling on solid ground, the machine landed on a pond hidden by the snow. The machine tilted then something hit the ground with unspeakable force and snow and dirt flew everywhere. Then came fire and smoke, and as the machine seemed to disintegrate before his eyes, he caught sight of a man strapped to a chair.

Forgetting his terror, he bounded down the slope. The dogs ran beside him, but the loud noise of the machine crashing had frightened them. They stayed close to him, their ears laid back.

In front of the machine he hesitated, but only for an instant. He kicked at the metal and glass bits and reached in. The man had tied himself to the chair and Kell didn't know how to pull off the strap. Choking, he drew back then noticed that the man wore a knife strapped to his leg. He took the knife and cut the straps, dragging the man to safety.

Another man lay in the debris, but Kell couldn't get to him in time. While he watched, helpless to do anything, the flying machine slid under the ice and disappeared into the black waters. The ice beneath his feet cracked ominously and he backed away, still holding the survivor in his arms. He glanced at him. This man still lived, but a huge gash bled freely on the side of his head. He surely had more injuries, but right now he had to get him to the village. He opened his jacket and tore a strip off his shirt, using it to staunch the man's wound.

Kell tied the strip tightly around the man's head. Then he whistled for the dogs, slung the man over his shoulder and started toward the tent. Allie would not be happy about going to the village, but they had to take the wounded man to safety.

Chapter Eight

Allie and Kell managed to lift the unconscious man onto the dogsled. Kell harnessed the dogs while Allie explained what a helicopter was, and how it worked. His blood turned to ice water in his veins, and he couldn't stop thinking of the smoke and the noise, and the sight of the machine vanishing beneath the ice, carrying its macabre load with it. That had been worse than any nightmare, worse than the elders' stories of dragons.

"Please, Allie, say no more about it." He faced her, his shoulders tense. Then he nodded toward the front of the sled. "The dogs can't pull you and the man both, and you cannot keep up with me. Set up the tent and the stove, and wait until I come back for you."

She nodded, her face white, and took the tent off the sled. "You don't speak their language."

"They will see that he is hurt." Kell didn't want to leave her, but the trail led uphill back to the village and the dogs would be too tired. "I will be back as soon as I can. I will leave him with the old woman who rented us a room. She will know what to do."

Allie nodded. "Remember, tell them it was a helicopter." She held up two fingers. "And there were two men. They will want to get the other man's body."

"I will remember." He leaned over and caught her arm. Pulling her close, he kissed her hard on the mouth. Longing shot through him, sharp as a knife. Her lips trembled, and he nuzzled her neck. "I must go."

"Hurry back."

Kell called to the dogs and they set off, leaning into their harnesses. Because of last night's snowfall, the snow was deep and the path rose sharply. Once past the ridge it should be easier. He plodded behind the sled, going as fast as he could, keeping hold of the sled but careful not to slow the dogs.

After an hour he stopped and wiped his face. Stomping his feet and blowing on his hands to warm himself up, he glanced at the man in the sled. The makeshift bandage was soaked and blood trickled down his cheek. His color looked bad, and he still breathed in shallow gasps. Not good signs. Kell frowned, then his gaze fell upon the brazier. Allie had taken the tent but had forgotten the brazier. Cursing, he looked behind him. If he turned back, the man might die. If he went on, Allie could freeze.

At that moment, the man uttered a low groan.

"By Belenus!" He had to get to the village. Then he would borrow the snowmobile and rush back to Allie as fast as he could. She would be too cold, he figured, to argue. He only hoped she had the sense to get in the tent and stay there until he got back. Did she have her medicine bag with her? He was sure she did, and inside her bag were the tiny magic sticks called matches. Allie would most likely be just fine.

Calmer now, he called to the dogs, encouraging them with his voice. His legs ached and his lungs burned, but he had run farther distances than this. If only the snow wasn't so deep.

By the time the village came into sight, he was drenched with sweat. The modern clothes kept him almost too hot. He drove the dogs straight to the woman's house and pounded on her door. When she opened it, she let out a startled cry.

Kell pointed to the man in the sled. "Heller popper!" He held up two fingers and pointed again to the man. He had no idea if she understood, but he had to go get Allie. He lifted the man off the sled and looked at the old woman.

Her mouth opened and shut, then she held the door opened and motioned for him to take the man to her dining room. Kell laid him on the table then, bowing to the woman, he left.

The dogs could hardly walk. Exhausted, they limped into the dog trader's yard, and relief washed through Kell when he saw the man's snowmobile parked in the back.

He couldn't waste time explaining. Already his muscles had started to stiffen with cold. He pounded on the door and waited until the man came out. Then he motioned to the dogs and to the snowmobile. He shook his head in frustration at not being able to speak his language. The only words that popped into his mind were "There's a brand-new car in my future" and other commercial refrains. For some reason, he didn't think that would help.

He made the sign of turning a key in the lock and pointed again to the snowmobile. The man looked surprised and spoke. Mixed in the words, Kell caught Allie's name.

Kell nodded. "Allie. Heller popper. There's no brand-new car in his future."

The dog trader said something else and disappeared into his house. When he came back out with the keys, Kell breathed a sigh of relief. He bowed then rushed to the snowmobile and started it. He drove off, trying not to notice that the sky had darkened again and the wind had started to pick up.

By the time he got back to the tent, another storm threatened. "Allie!" he cried. He grabbed the stove off the snowmobile and ran to the tent. "Are you all right?"

* * * *

Allie blew on her fingers and rubbed her arms. How had she forgotten the camp stove? In her panic and rush to get the wounded man to the village, she had forgotten to take the stove off the sled. She didn't have a bite to eat and no matches left in her purse, so making a fire was out of the question. The early spring weather wasn't as bitterly cold as winter, but the chill penetrated the tent without the little stove to keep it at bay.

Finally, she decided to go to the site of the helicopter crash and see for herself what had happened. Exercise would keep her warm. She set out across the field, up the slope, and stood at the top of the ridge. Below her, a gaping hole in the ice marked where the helicopter had landed, but there was no sign of the helicopter. The pond must be much deeper than she thought. Perhaps it was a sinkhole, in which case recovering the helicopter would be next to impossible.

She glanced at the sky. A heavy snowfall would even cover the signs of the crash. Already a frosty crust of thin ice formed on the pond. Shadows moved over the snow and she glanced at the sky. Clouds piled on the horizon. She shivered, looking in the direction Kell had taken. A lump formed in her throat. She hoped he would return soon. Walking briskly, she headed back to the tent.

She had only been there a minute, it seemed, before she heard the sound of a snowmobile. Heart pounding, she peered out of the tent. Kell! He saw her and waved then carried the stove into the tent.

"Are you all right?" he asked, worry in his voice.

"I'm fine." She smiled and managed to hide her chattering teeth, but she couldn't hide her sigh of contentment when Kell lit the stove and warmth flooded the tent.

"You were cold. I'm sorry. I should have turned back." He took her hands in his. "Did you not have your magic matches?"

"I didn't have any left. No, you did what was right. I'm fine, really. Do you have anything to eat?"

"I brought back some supplies. The weather will change tonight. I'm afraid another storm is on its way, but it shouldn't last long."

Allie grinned. "You could make a fortune working at the weather station."

Kell remembered the talking torso on the black television box and shuddered. "No, thank you."

She peered at him, suddenly worried. "You're flushed.

And your shirt is sopping wet! Kell, you have to get out of those wet clothes."

"If you insist." He gave her a leer and she rolled her eyes as he peeled off his shirt and trousers with exaggerated slowness.

Naked, he stood in front of the stove and warmed his hands and toes. His skin glowed in the red heat, and when he turned to her, her breath caught in her throat. God, he was handsome. In the village, women had stared at him in open admiration, and Allie knew what they had felt. He had broad shoulders, narrow hips, and muscular arms and legs. His brown hair curled loosely around his head, and his eyes, with their long lashes and arching eyebrows, were bright with...fever? She frowned and put her hand on his forehead.

"You're burning up!"

"I don't feel so good," he admitted. "But when you're near me, I feel better. I hurried to get back to you." Taking her in his arms, he bent over and nuzzled her neck. His skin burned with fever.

She pulled away. "Hold on, let me get you some aspirin."

She took the bottle and opened it, and told him how to swallow it with a gulp of water. He choked once or twice and started to cough. His cough sounded dreadfully deep and hoarse. Disquiet gave way to fear.

"I have to get you to a doctor. Come get your clothes back on. We're going to the village."

"Clothes back on? I don't think so." He grabbed her and spun her around. "Bend over, Allie. My need has made my cock as strong as iron, and I long to stab you with my sword."

"Fever doesn't agree with you," gasped Allie. Then she noticed his erection. That was all it took to make her knees go weak. *Damn, he cannot be serious.* She should be getting him to a doctor.

"Off with the clothes, woman," he ordered, his voice low and caressing.

A shiver ran over her body. "All right, but afterward we go to the village and get you some antibiotics."

That gave him a pause. "What word is that?"

"Modern medicine. You'll see. It works like magic."

His eyebrows lifted in surprise. "I didn't think magic existed in this time. All I've seen is science and technology."

Now it was Allie's turn to be surprised. "That's very observant of you."

He snorted. "Well, the same can't be said of you. Look, woman. Don't you notice anything?"

His cock stood straight up, seemingly pointing straight at her.

She gulped. She stripped off her clothes, helped along by Kell, who couldn't seem to get her pants off fast enough. While they still caught around her ankles, he moaned and slipped his hands between her thighs, fingers searching for her cleft. Then he pushed her to her hands and knees, mounting her with the urgency of a stallion.

She couldn't stop the cry of pure lust that burst from her throat. A gush of moisture heated her cunt, but when his cock thrust into her, she gasped. It burned as if on fire. He arched over her, his hands clasping her shoulders, his thighs pushing against hers with every long, deep thrust. His breath came in short, harsh gasps and he began to quiver.

Liquid fire filled her as he shot his seed into her. As it flooded her, her cunt contracted violently, drawing a whimper from her. Black spots danced in front of her eyes and her whole body seemed to turn inside out. Kell's cock twitched and he slid off her with a groan and collapsed at her side. The cool air startled her and she touched his forehead. It burned her hand and she drew a frightened breath.

What was I thinking?

She had to get Kell to a doctor—now!

* * * *

"He was raving about a brand-new car?" Allie tried to keep the worry out of her voice, but it wavered anyhow.

Kell and she had managed to get back, despite the storm. The wind had whipped ice crystals into her face and had chilled her to the bone, but it hadn't quenched Kell's fever. He had sat on the snowmobile and had just barely managed to hang on to her.

She had convinced the dog trader to take back the snowmobile, dogs and sled in exchange for some cash, and she'd gotten the room back at the old lady's boarding house. Then she had managed to find a doctor to come out in the storm. When he had finished examining Kell, his expression was grave.

The verdict was pneumonia. They had set up an oxygen tent and Kell had become agitated, convinced he was trapped under the plastic. Finally, the doctor had to give him a sedative.

"He should be moved to a hospital," the doctor told her, shaking his head.

"He doesn't have any insurance," Allie said. How was she going to pay for all this? Exhausted and worried, she called her bank. That's when she found out her account had been frozen.

The woman who had rented them a room insisted they stay, anyway. The boy Kell had found was her grandson. She even managed to persuade the doctor to continue treating Kell here, at her house.

But Allie was frantic, worried about Kell, and frightened that the police would show up any minute and take her away from him.

"He said your name, something about a hello popper, then he said 'a brand-new car in my future,' clear as day." The dog trader patted her hand. "Don't fret now. Doc knows how to treat pneumonia. He'll be up and around in no time."

Allie smiled gratefully. The dog trader's name was Doug.

His wife was Amy, and their two boys Doug Jr. and Brody. The old woman who had rented them a room was Doug's mother, Mrs. Willig. She had started to think of them as her friends, and she desperately needed friends right now.

"What about the man who was in the helicopter accident?"

"He woke up and seems all right. Doc has an eye on him too. Did you want to see him?"

Allie almost said no then she realized that would seem strange, so she swallowed and said, "Of course."

Doug glanced at Amy and she shrugged in that way that married couples have when they've been together so long they can read each other's minds. A sudden pang of jealousy mixed with sorrow pricked Allie.

"Allie, where is your friend Kell from? When he speaks his language it almost sounds like… Well, I hope you're not going to think I'm being nosy, but it sounds like Welsh."

"Do you speak Welsh?" Allie sighed. The questions would start and she didn't have any idea how to answer them.

"Matter of fact, my grandmother was Welsh." Doug shrugged. "I don't want to pry or anything."

"It's all right, I have to tell someone sometime." She plucked at the tablecloth. "He's actually almost Welsh. He's Celt, and he speaks Latin and Celt, or Keltoi, as he calls it."

"Latin and Celt?" Amy raised her eyebrows. "Those are dead languages. How is that possible?"

"Because he's been frozen for thousands of years." Allie braced herself. The three people sitting at the table with her, Doug, Amy and Mrs. Willig, stared at her with identical expressions of disbelief on their faces.

"Can you run that by us again?" Doug shook his head, took a sip of his beer and leaned forward. "Not that we don't believe you, but you realize it sounds kind of…"

"Hard to believe," finished Amy.

Allie took a deep breath. "Russian scientists found him in a glacier buried under the ice about two years ago. They gave him to the Americans who started to study him when, after someone sent a jolt of electricity through his body, his heart started beating. The scientists called in the military and they transferred him to a secret base not too far from here."

"Yeah, we all know about it. The secret base no one is supposed to know about." Amy rolled her eyes. "So they woke up Kell. Where do you fit in, and how come you're not still on the base?"

"I specialize in dead languages. I'm his translator. And we left because of this." Allie pulled the fax out of her pocket and smoothed it carefully.

Doug examined it, Amy reading aloud over his shoulder. Mrs. Willig uttered a shocked cry when she heard the word dissect.

All three started speaking at once.

"No way!" gasped Amy.

"It's scandalous!" said Mrs. Willig, her eyes flashing in anger.

"I can't believe it!" Doug pounded his fist on the table. "I won't let anyone harm the man who saved my son."

A smile tugged Allie's lips. Though she knew Kell hadn't saved anyone, he had only tracked the little boy down. "Thank you."

"But why is your bank account frozen?" Amy wanted to know.

"I stole more than just Kell from the base. I took snowsuits and a snowmobile. If they catch me, I guess that's what I'll be accused of. I can't imagine they can prosecute me for saving Kell's life."

"Are you saying that the Army wants to cut Kell up in pieces and that the Ski-Doo that fell into the lake was military property so you're wanted for theft?" Mrs. Willig set her teacup on the saucer with a clatter. "Doug, you get on the phone right now and call that lawyer woman who used to go to school with you."

"Ma—"

"Don't you 'Ma' me. Get on that phone and tell her to help these people out. It isn't right when a man is hunted like a wild animal. He's got to have rights, don't he? Even if he don't have a birth certificate or nationality." Mrs. Willig glared at Doug. "I thought I told you to get on that telephone."

"Yes'm."

Doug left the room and Allie smiled weakly at Amy and Mrs. Willig. "There's more. I think that the man in the helicopter was out looking for us. When the Army gets wind of the accident, they'll send a whole battalion, and maybe they'll try to pin the accident on Kell, anything to get their hands on him."

Mrs. Willig patted Allie's hand. "Don't fret now, dear. First they'll have to find him." She gave a wink. "Folk have a habit of just disappearing into thin air around here, I do declare."

* * * *

Everything ached and fire ran through his veins, scorching him from the inside out. Kell moaned, trying to open his eyes, but the light blinded him, sending stabbing pains to his skull.

"I'm sorry. Let me turn that off," Allie's voice came from beside him.

A cool hand touched his forehead and he sighed. The light dimmed and he managed to look around.

He lay in the bedroom, and to his relief the television box had been removed. He vaguely recalled having a fit when he'd seen it, and a tremor ran through him. Rarely did his fear get the best of him. He must be dying.

"I go to join my ancestors," he said, figuring he had better break the news to Allie while he could still talk.

Her eyebrows rose, but she didn't dissolve into fits of tears.

For some reason, this vexed him. "Don't you care?"

"Of course I do! But you're getting better," she said, her cool hand stroking his cheek.

"Better than what?" He frowned at her. "I want you to put my body on a boat and send it to the sea." An idea struck him. "Can you put it on a boat with a motor attached to it?"

Her mouth twitched. If he didn't know better, he would think she was about to laugh. Instead she cleared her throat and said, "The motor attached to the boat or to your body?"

There, he had seen it. A definite grin. How could she be so heartless? His body burned with fever. Everyone knew that fever and chest pains and coughing meant death. He could hardly breathe. Well, she would regret it when he'd passed into the land of his ancestors, riding in the boat with the motor...*wait a minute*. He scowled at her. "Attached to the boat, of course."

She nodded seriously and said, "Tell me more. What else should we do?"

Was there a hint of laughter in her voice? She wouldn't dare. This was a sacred moment. He tried to speak in a haughty tone but a coughing fit shook him, and he spent a few minutes getting his breath back. There, that should make her more attentive.

"You have to make it go as fast as possible, and load the boat with gifts for my ancestors and for my shade to use in the other world."

She nodded. "Gifts. Like what?"

"Coffee and chocolate," he said.

A muscle twitched in her jaw. "Chocolate?"

"Exactly." He could just imagine his ancestors when they got a taste of that chocolate. "Better put a lot."

"What else?"

He tried to remember the ceremony. "Don't forget to set the boat on fire before sending it off to sea."

She held up her hand and ticked off the details on her fingers. "Body inside boat. Motor on boat. Chocolate...lots of chocolate...in boat, as well. Set it on fire, start the motor and send the boat with the body, and the chocolate, off to ancestors as fast as it can possibly go." She smiled brightly. "Did I miss anything?"

"How can you be so heartless?" His voice broke, and his heart must have broken, as well. He lay there dying, and the woman he loved above all others thought it a joke.

"Kell!" The tenderness in her voice startled him.

He looked at her and saw tears in her eyes. About time.

She took his hands in his. "You're not dying. It's true that you were very ill, but the doctor says you're on the mend. He says you'll be up and around in a few days." She shook her head and the tears spilled over her lashes and rolled down her cheeks. "How could you ever think I don't care for you? I love you, Kell. You mean the world to me."

"You teased me." He knew he sounded childish but his heart was too light to care. She loved him. She had said so. "You love me?"

"Yes." She cried now, huge sobs shaking her even as she smiled at him.

"I tell you I'm dying and you laugh. I say I love you and you cry. I'll never understand you, woman."

* * * *

Allie packed their bag, Kell sitting on the foot of her bed watching. Doug had been as good as his word, and his friend—a lawyer in Toronto—had come almost right away. The lawyer specialized in human rights, and she had immediately drafted an appeal to the Canadian government for Kell for political asylum. In the meantime, the Inuit granted him citizenship. He had his own passport now. The best thing about that had been putting his date of birth as 'The Year of the Swans', 390 BC.

The worst thing about it was that Allie had to go to court and face charges. The United States Army had arrested her for theft and vandalism, as well as breach of contract. She had made a huge dent in her savings and she'd lost her job, but as she looked at Kell, she knew it had been worth it.

Kell was free. The U.S. Army had no claim on his person whatsoever, as the lawyer pointed out. He had never signed any contract to be anyone's guinea pig, and the bills they had sent him for medical treatment were dismissed on the same grounds. The Russians who had sold his body to the U.S. Army were no more responsible. Their contract had stipulated one frozen cadaver. Kell obviously was no cadaver.

As far as recovering the helicopter, the Army sent trucks and winches, and managed to salvage part of the wreckage, but the other body was not recovered. As Allie had speculated, the pond was a sinkhole and dropped nearly straight down for over a hundred feet.

The Army had also taken the man Kell had saved into their care. His name was Fred Grafferty, and he had insisted on thanking Kell in person. The missing man, a certain Bruce Steele, had never been found. His body had vanished somewhere in the depths of the partially frozen sinkhole.

"Kell!" Doug stuck his head in the doorway, a wide grin on his face. "Guess what? You've been invited to speak at the Toronto cultural center, all expenses paid, chic hotel and everything. I just got the fax from your lawyer. International television and radio coverage. You're official, man! You're going to be a star!"

Kell turned to Allie for help. His English was still limited to terms about brand-new cars, guns, food and some swear words so far. He could ask for chocolate and coffee, and tell Doug his truck was cool, but this was beyond him.

Allie raised her eyebrows. "You're going to be a very wealthy man, Kell. Your lawyer will make sure you get paid for your appearances, and several television programs want to feature you. You're booked solid for years to come, all over the world."

Kell peered at her from beneath lowered lashes. "So why do you look so unhappy, Allie?"

Startled, she put down the T-shirt she had been folding and rubbed her forehead. She had been trying to act happy for Kell, but he saw right through her.

"Tell me." He didn't ask, he ordered.

"You haven't seen very many other women..." She had no idea how to explain the knots of jealousy in her chest. When he saw the city women and compared them to her, he would see how small and uninteresting she really was.

His eyebrows shot up. "Other women? Allie, do you think I seek another woman?" He started to chuckle, then saw her expression and stopped. He reached out, caught her wrist and drew her to him. "Allie of the flame-colored tresses. Allie of the dimples." He kissed her and sat her on his knee. "I have no interest in other women. Especially the emaciated ones your culture seems to worship." He pinched her nipple and she uttered a squeak of surprise.

"Kell!" Relief flooded her. He wasn't saying that just to make her feel better.

A spark of humor twinkled in his eyes. "I have a plan. I wanted to talk to you about it, so listen, woman." He wrapped his arms around her and leaned his chin on her shoulder. "With my wealth, I plan to buy land here in the north. I need to spend time here, for it is my element. You need me when you are with me here. I protect you and care for you. Here, I am your survival. But we must spend time in your world too. And there, you protect me and guide me. In my mind, ours is the perfect partnership. Each of us has what the other requires." He paused and took her hands in his. "Our children will have the best of both worlds."

Allie's heart pounded and tears pricked her eyes. "Oh, Kell, you are wonderful."

He grinned. "I know." Then he grew serious again. "Allie, when I woke up in this world, I felt as if my very soul had vanished. As if my life had turned to the dust of time and I had nothing to look forward to. As if all I cared for was behind me. You taught me to live again. You gave me back the will to live, the need to laugh, and to love again. You are the woman I choose above all others. Will you be my heart-mate, Allie, and marry me at the spring solstice?"

"Yes." No hesitation. She kissed him, her lips lingering on his. Then a thought struck her and a shiver ran down her spine. She hated flying. Hopefully Kell wouldn't be too terrified.

* * * *

"This is incredible. Look, Allie, look! Why are you shaking? Take your hands away from your eyes. The sunset is amazing from up here. The houses are all tiny. There are lights everywhere. I can see car lights on that road, and there is another plane up here with us. Over there! Can you see it?" Kell couldn't understand why Allie trembled so much. His whole being sang with a sort of fierce, wild joy as the plane had taken off. When the ground had dropped away, he had stared, incredulous, thrilled beyond measure. Man could fly!

Allie gripped his arm so tightly it hurt. "I hate flying," she said, her teeth chattering.

Kell frowned. How strange. Forever had man stared into the sky and dreamed of flying. He tapped her shoulder. "Over there is a lake, and the cars are the size of ants!"

"Leave me alone!" She cowered in her chair, hands over her eyes.

Perplexed, he scanned the cabin. Were all the voyagers so timid? The section of the plane they were in was nearly empty. Allie had called it 'first class'. He twisted around to peer behind them. Nobody else appeared concerned. One man read his journal, a woman sipped a glass of water, and another woman dozed, a blanket on her lap. He searched and found a blanket on the seat next to him. The sun finished setting. It was dusk now, and the inside the plane had gone dark, with only small pinpoints of light coming from the ceiling. He found it strangely restful. Allie, on the other hand, was still trembling and had her eyes tightly closed.

"I know what to do," he whispered. He draped the blanket over Allie's lap, then he slipped to the floor and ducked under the blanket. It was a tight squeeze, but he managed.

Allie stiffened, but he pushed her knees apart and hooked his fingers into her underpants.

They were so silky and lacy. He loved to touch them. Even more, he loved to touch Allie's soft skin and her sex. He tugged off her underwear and she reached under the blanket to grab his wrist.

"Stop!" she whispered.

"Hush, woman!" He pushed her knees farther apart and stroked the soft curls framing her sex. He put his hand between her thighs, keeping her knees wide, then he started teasing her with just the lightest of touches, getting close to her labia then darting away. Soon she relaxed her legs, arched her hips, and uttered a soft, plaintive moan.

Moisture gathered in her folds, and he dipped his finger into her sex. Under the blanket, in total darkness, he moved higher, pressing his mouth to her cunt and finding her clitoris with his tongue. As her clit stiffened, so did his cock, growing heavy and pressing against his pants. Her musky scent filled his nostrils, exciting him even more.

His cock ached, and he reached down to adjust his pants. Allie groaned and squirmed closer to his mouth, her juices wetting his chin. Kell felt like groaning too. In a minute he would explode. He wanted to plunge his cock into Allie's sex and satisfy them both, but he knew her society had taboos about sex in public places. Even during the solstice festivals Allie had told him there were no more orgies here. More was the pity. He would have loved to show Allie off.

He tried to imagine a solstice without an orgy, to calm his raging need, but all he could think of was rolling over and over in long, fragrant grass with Allie naked in his arms, his cock wedged tightly into her cunt, while the hot sun rays of the summer solstice covered their bodies like warm honey.

Speaking of honey... He kept his head down and let his tongue tickle and tease her clit until it throbbed. Sliding one, then two fingers into her passage, he found it wet and swollen. Her flesh gripped his fingers and her body quivered. A flood of heat surged through him and she reached down and grabbed his hands, pushing them farther into her body. Her hips rose and fell, and suddenly she pushed him away and got up.

Dazed, Kell peeled the blanket off and stared at her. Eyes bright, face flushed, Allie pointed to a door. "Meet me in there."

She teetered to the door and slipped inside. Kell glanced around. No one paid them any attention. Hiding his erection with his hands, he got to his feet then walked a bit unsteadily down the aisle and slipped into the tiny room.

Allie locked the door behind him and before he could say anything, she grabbed him and kissed him hungrily. Her heart pounded against his chest, and her nipples hardened into twin pebbles. He unbuttoned her blouse and pulled her lacy bra off her shoulders. With a muffled groan he took her nipple in his mouth and tugged at it.

Allie unzipped his pants and pushed them off his hips, freeing his hard cock. Her hands wrapped around it and he thrust, his need making him gasp for breath. The counter behind her seemed the right height. He lifted Allie and set her on it, parting her knees and guiding his cock into her tight pussy.

The vibrations from the plane ran through his body, and he felt them as he drove into Allie's cunt, his cock slipping and sliding into her slick flesh. Her hot, velvety passage squeezed his cock, his need mounting as his balls contracted.

He buried his face into Allie's shoulder and a harsh cry tore from his throat while his seed shot from him. Grasping Allie's waist tightly, he held her as close as he could while his hips drove his cock into her. She uttered a cry and tremors ran through her body.

Then a strange dinging sounded and a woman spoke from behind him. Kell whirled around, expecting to see someone, but the voice emanated from one of those things called a speaker. He sighed and nuzzled Allie's breast.

"We have to go sit down. We're about to land," she said.

Kell kissed her. "Here, let me help you down." He loved

how the faucets worked in modern bathrooms, and he quickly washed himself. He insisted on washing Allie, although it got him hard again. Pressing his cock down and trying to make improvements in the way his pants fit, he made his way back to his seat. Allie followed a minute later.

He stared out of the window as they landed, while Allie clutched at his arm and chanted prayers. Some things never changed, he mused, when the plane touched down. The stewardess asked them if they had enjoyed their flight and they couldn't help laughing.

Chapter Nine

Steele heard a steady thumping first. Softly, then louder, until he suddenly realized that the sound was his own heartbeat and his eyes flew open. His whole body twitched and he had the sudden sensation of falling. Too much light dazzled his eyes, his chest hurt, and, when he gasped and dragged a gulp of air into his lungs, he had the impression he breathed fire. The pain wrenched a cry from his throat, and each movement sent stabbing knives of agony through his body.

Voices sounded above and all around him. He tried to fix his attention upon them to hear what they said. Before he could make sense out of the noises, at first far too loud for his ears, they quieted. Silence. The voices had vanished. Or, more likely, he had become accustomed to the noise the same way his eyes had slowly become accustomed to the light. What at first had dazzled him revealed itself to be soft, halogen lights above his head. What he had taken for a buzz of voices turned into the steady hum of what appeared to be an air conditioner affixed to the wall.

He gazed around. White walls, large windows, floods of light and chrome machines he had never seen glittering beneath the lamps. A hospital? He tried to think. He had never been sick a day in his life. But whose life? Who was he? He closed his eyes and tried to gather his thoughts.

Nothing. Everything was blank. Or wait... A campfire. A cheerful fire, steaks grilling on the coals, and taking a drink of something cold and delicious...beer. A beer! He knew those words. Beer, steaks, campfire… Okay, he had made some progress.

He opened his eyes again. He lay in a bed, and for some reason, his arms and legs had been fastened to the bed so that he couldn't move. He pulled gently, then harder, trying to tug himself free. The effort caused him pain and sweat prickled on his brow.

"Is anyone here?" he called out. His voice sounded rusty and cracked. He cleared his throat and tried again. "Hello? Is anyone here?"

Footsteps sounded in the hallway and the door slid upward. He blinked. Then someone came in the doorway and his breath caught in his throat. A woman with long, flame-red hair and delicate seashell coloring walked up to him. She looked down at him, and her dark blue eyes filled with gentle compassion.

"You are awake. That's good. Don't panic, please, nothing will hurt you here." She spoke in a soft murmur.

"Where am I?" He wanted to get up and walk around. He must have been lying in this position for ages. His legs and arms could hardly bend. They were as stiff as wooden boards. He could practically hear them creak when he moved. But why was he tied down?

"You are on Tazi Prime. We brought you here when your heart started to beat again on its own. The doctors were quite thrilled." She cocked her head. "Shall I take your restraints off?"

"Please." Relief flooded through him, although he hadn't understood half of what she had said. Had he had a heart attack? Was that why his heart had stopped beating? Why couldn't he remember that? What hospital was Tazi Prime? He had never heard of it.

She touched his fetters and they disappeared. Neat trick, that. He swallowed hard. The thought he might be dreaming occurred to him.

"You are free to walk around this room. Please do not leave, as you will need a great deal of education before you can integrate into our society."

He rubbed his head. "Look, uh... I'm sorry, what is your name?"

She smiled gravely. "My name is F-69. I am your companion and teacher."

"Eff-sixty-nine?" he faltered. "That's not a name, it's a number. Is this the Army? Is that your...?" The word escaped him. "Your registration number?" Things trickled back.

"No, this is not the Army and that is not my registration. My serial number. That is correct. My organic parts are the same as yours, but my brain is a Deca-myria III, the best you can buy at this time. Of course, in another Rev I will probably be obsolete." She tossed back her long hair and smiled ruefully, her blue eyes twinkling.

"Rev?" he croaked.

"Revolution of Capitol Planet around its sun. Equal to point eleven of what you called a year." She beamed at him. "Any other questions?"

Deca-myria? Organic parts? Capitol Planet? Nothing she said made sense, and his memories seemed locked in a small room with a can of beer. Something had to give him the key to his memories. My name! Maybe that will help. "Do you know my name?"

"Your name is Bruce Steele. You are thirty-two years old and you are in peak physical condition, thanks to the amazing properties of cryogenics and our technology." Her smile widened. "Does that help you?"

Bruce Steele. Steele. He nodded. *Steele, he went by that name.* The door to his recollections cracked open, letting a thin slice of bright light through.

Without warning the door was flung wide and a flood of memories assailed him, knocking him back on the bed. His head slammed into the pillow as visions flashed in his mind. Visions and sounds battered him. Bruce Steele. Born to Ed and Janet Steele. Growing up in a small town. Playing with his friends. A shy boy who loved camping.

121

Fishing with his father. School. Graduation and getting his car. The Army. War in a faraway land. Coming home. Tracking. Working as a game warden then as a detective. His parents' death in a car crash. Tracking. Working for the Army and tracking people lost in the mountains. Getting married. Getting divorced. Tracking. The last image took place in a helicopter. The snow, the landing, the jolt and sudden fear... The deep darkness then nothing.

Steele lay on his bed, heart pounding as if he had just run the mile. He had been a professional tracker. He had died. No, he'd been frozen in that deep lake. He knew what the word cryogenics meant. Deep, ice-induced sleep. How long had he slept? He searched his brain for something to give him a clue. Nothing. He squeezed his eyes shut then opened them.

"How long have I been asleep?"

She smiled broadly. "Excellent question! Your first test has been passed with flying colors. You didn't fall apart and turn into a blithering..."

Steele caught her wrist in his hand. "Just answer the question."

A flash of hurt surprise crossed her face, then she sighed and said, "You have been 'asleep', as you call it, for six thousand and thirteen years, five months, six days and..." She glanced at her watch. "Twelve hours and fifteen seconds."

Steele let go of her and slumped back in his bed. "Such a long time," he whispered. He chewed that over for a few moments, but, to be honest, six thousand years was too vast. It just didn't sink in. Well, he would think about it later. He looked at the beautiful android. "Are you always so precise?"

Her expression cleared. "Yes. Second test passed with flying colors. You didn't fall to pieces and run screaming around the room when you heard how much time had passed. You are by far our most accommodating patient—"

"Excuse me." Steele held his hand up. "There are others

like myself?"

"Of course. We get some from all over the galaxy. Tazi Prime is a space station specializing in the art of cryogenics. It was specifically built for long-distance space travel. We send bodies to sleep for centuries while they are sent to another destination. Cryogenics is a very important business and area of study. You have been asleep for six thousand years, long enough to travel the whole length of the known galaxy. You arrived here a few days ago, and I have been monitoring you closely ever since." She smiled broadly. "You are our star patient and by far our oldest subject."

Steele tried not to panic. He had never panicked before in his life, but right now, a good scream and a run around the room would do him good. Instead, he ran his hand through his hair while his thoughts whirled.

Six thousand years. Six thousand… He grabbed a handful of hair and yanked. "Ouch!" That hurt. This was not a dream.

"Are you all right?" The woman peered at him with a worried expression.

He needed a stiff drink. No, that would be a mistake. He had used alcohol once before as a crutch and he would never start that again. But he needed something. His throat was dry and scratchy, and his head hurt. "I don't suppose you have anything to drink? Something not too alcoholic. Or a beer. That would be great."

F-69 nodded happily. "You are amazing, Mr. Steele. No hysterics at all. I didn't have to use my tranquilizer dart once." She grinned and held up a gadget that looked like a tiny plastic water pistol.

Tranquilizer dart? Well, he supposed some people might get upset after waking up sixty centuries after they'd fallen asleep. Right now, he was just dazed, and only half believed this wasn't some sort of a dream. Upset would come later. When he had the energy to scream. Or when he could stop shaking.

"Mr. Steele, here, let me rub your head a little. I find it relaxes people."

Her fingers were soothing as she gently stroked his temples. She massaged his head and neck until he loosened up. When he stopped trembling, he felt much better and things didn't seem so bad after all.

"Thank you."

She gave him another thousand-watt smile. "I'm sorry, we don't have beer today. But I'll see that you have it tomorrow. If you'd like, I have some iced frinton tea. How does that sound?"

"Er, frinton?"

"It's a bit like mint. You'll love it."

"Fine." Anything would help straighten out his thoughts. He hoped. He looked at the tranquilizer gun again. Maybe a shot of that wouldn't be too bad. He winced. "Can I have some now, please?"

"Yes, of course. I will get you a glass of frinton tea right away. Why don't you watch some holo-vision and get acquainted with this era? We have tapes made to show our patients when they wake up that explain how their world differs from ours, to get you used to society."

F-69 was starting to get on his nerves. She was like a perky Barbie doll come to life. Did she ever stop smiling? "Sure, good idea."

He searched for the television or the remote control.

But F-69 simply said, "Holo-vision tape one for Mr. Steele, please." And instantly a cloud materialized at the foot of his bed and took the form of a large, transparent cube. Inside, a man's head appeared and he started to talk.

Steele jumped about a foot off the bed. He had heard of holograms, but this one had them all beat.

"Normally they are as big as the wall, but we made this one smaller so that you wouldn't be afraid." F-69 then went to the wall and pushed a small button. "One frinton tea," she said.

"Er, won't you join me?" Steele glanced at the hologram,

where a man pointed at what seemed to be a 1960s room in a house and showed how all the furniture had changed throughout the centuries. As he watched, a refrigerator morphed into a tiny button on the wall. The button was in every room and was connected to the kitchen. From anywhere in the house, one could push the button, order a cold drink, and be served.

He watched as a small opening appeared in the wall in front of F-69, and she reached in and took out a glass of pale blue liquid. *Cool. I could get used to that.* She handed it to him and he took a sip. Refreshing. Light. Strange. A mix between mint tea and something that smelled like roses. Steele sniffed at the drink and shrugged. It was quite nice, actually.

On the holo-vision the man had just finished talking about the vacuum cleaner. He walked out of the house and pointed.

The man in the holo-vision smiled and said, "Next, we see the progress the car has made..."

Whoa! It flies! He wanted one of those babies.

Chapter Ten

After three days, Steele started to get cabin fever. There were no windows so he was plagued with claustrophobia. He was used to being outdoors most of the time, and this enforced confinement annoyed him. He couldn't leave his room because of some sort of time-lag quarantine. Supposedly he had a few germs that had unfrozen and had woken up at the same time his body had and he had to wait until they were gone. F-69 explained everything carefully — of course — and he had medicine to take. He didn't complain, and he didn't panic. But he was bored. Plus, he was horny. One side effect of being thawed out was an enhanced sensory perception in the extremities. His hands and feet tingled constantly and a low electrical charge seemed to run through his body.

F-69 explained it was simply the body's way of adapting to his circulation, and he didn't mind, except that his cock tingled all day long and it got hard at the slightest touch.

He felt like a school kid with a hormone problem. To make things worse, F-69 trotted around in a skimpy suit that showed her curves to perfection. Not only did she have a cleavage that seemed to beg him to dip his tongue or finger into its creamy cleft, but her skirt sometimes rode high enough on her thighs so that he caught glimpses of her rounded buttocks.

For the third time that day he had to excuse himself from his 'future' lessons and go into the bathroom to jerk off.

She knocked on the door. "Are you all right? Did something disagree with you?"

Steele gritted his teeth. "No. I'm fine."

"Well, I have to go out for a while. I'll try to be back in time for lesson number thirty-six C. You'll enjoy it. It's all about our electoral system and how we choose our delegates to the Federation."

How thrilling. "Take your time." He waited until he heard the door shut, and he peered out. No one. Alone at last. With his hard-on. His cock was stiff as a marble rod. His balls contracted, and he closed his eyes and accidentally leaned against the refrigerator. Or at least, he leaned against the small button.

A voice sounded from the wall, "Hel-lo. I. Am. The. Re-fri-gor-ator."

Steele jumped back. "I know that." He had no idea why the refrigerator sounded like the cliché of an old-fashioned robot, or he always answered the machine. He sighed.

"Would. You. Like. A. Beer?"

"Actually." Steele cleared his throat. "I'd like a melon."

"Wat-er-mel-on? Musk? Cant-a-loupe...?"

"Um, anything would be fine."

"Do. You. Want. It. Sliced. Or—?"

"No! No, thank you. Um, whole, please. Just leave it whole. Um, could you drill a hole in it, about so big?" He held his hands about three inches apart.

"I. Can-not. See. I. Am. A. Re-fri-gor-a-tor. What. Are. You. Go-ing. To. Do. With. The. Me-lon?"

"You don't want to know." Steele leaned his forehead against the wall and groaned.

"Do. You. Want. An-y-thing. Else. With. That?"

"No. Thank you."

The wall hummed and a little door slid open, revealing a plate with a small watermelon on it. Steele took the plate and looked around. Dinner usually came when F-69 ordered it, and he had no idea where the knives and forks were kept. No matter. He hurried into the bathroom and, using the pointed end of his toothbrush, dug a hole in the melon.

Not exactly a pussy sleeve, but close enough. He took his

cock out of his pants and, holding the melon, slid his cock into it. Seedless, thank God. He had forgotten to check. He'd been in such a hurry. The melon made a sucking sound as he thrust in and out. It tugged at his cock, and he pushed the melon harder. Then he pulled out. To his consternation, the melon had made a sort of vacuum around his penis and it stuck.

Nervously, he twisted it. Ouch. His cock stayed hard though. He was so horny he thought he would go cross-eyed, but what would happen if he came? He wasn't thinking clearly. Wait a minute. Would the vacuum get so strong it would give his cock a huge hickey? Holding the melon on his cock, he went into the living room to look for something to pry it off or cut it with. Or he would break it open by banging it on something hard. Well, if that worked, his cock should have split it asunder by now.

He hesitated, his cock throbbing, then the door opened and F-69 walked in. She stopped, and her beautiful blue eyes widened. A flush spread over her cheeks, and, to his consternation, she burst into tears and fled into his bathroom, slamming the door behind her.

He ran after her, awkwardly holding the melon, and knocked on the door. "Hey, I'm sorry. I was just... Hell. I just... I know it looks like I'm... But I'm not." He leaned his forehead against the door. "Okay. I am. But I got stuck, and now I can't get it off. Can you tell me where the knives are kept?"

The door swung inward and he pitched forward. F-69 caught him. His face pressed right into her cleavage and a surge of desire shot through his body. His cock throbbed in time to his heartbeat.

"It's not worth killing yourself about!" she cried.

"What are you talking about?" he spoke with his mouth on her soft skin.

"You said something about knives." Her voice took on a strange tone and she cleared her throat. "You're tickling me."

He blinked. His hand had slipped up her skirt and he cupped her buttocks. And his mouth had nudged her blouse down and had somehow found her nipple. It hardened as he sucked on it. His other hand still held the melon.

"Sorry." Steele managed to unglue his mouth from her nipple and stepped backward. He cleared his throat. "I just wanted the knife to get my melon off."

F-69 stood with her back propped against the wall, eyes opened wide. "Is that what you did with melons in your time?"

"Only when you were so horny you couldn't think straight," admitted Steele.

"Your face is all red. Are you embarrassed?"

"I'm several light years beyond embarrassed, yes. And as you can see, I'm so horny I could screw a melon. Help me get this off my cock."

"Help you what?"

Steele wondered if this was a new record for levels of shame. "It's stuck."

"Oh, a vacuum created by —"

"I know that." Steele tried to keep the edge of hysteria out of his voice. In a minute, he would explode and he wasn't sure what that would do to his hard-on inside the melon.

F-69 still hadn't tucked her breast back in her blouse, giving him high blood pressure. His cock gave another massive twinge.

"You poor thing." Her voice dropped to a purr and before he could react, she took the melon in her hands and pulled it apart with a loud cracking sound.

He took a step backward but she caught his belt buckle.

"Not so fast, Steele." The tip of her tongue touched her upper lip and she sighed. "I love melons."

Before he could formulate a reply, she had gotten to her knees and pulled his pants down to his ankles. Melon juice covered his cock and balls, and she licked it off, running her hot, velvety tongue over his skin. Sliding her mouth slowly and tightly over his cock, she gave a low, contented hum that vibrated from the tip of his toes to the top of his skull.

Steele closed his eyes and grabbed the door. Her mouth sucked him from the root to tip and back down again. Her lips held him firmly and her fingers tickled his balls and the insides of his thighs, and he knew that in precisely two point— *argh, not even!* His balls contracted and a huge jet of cum shot out of his cock. He groaned and held tightly to the door, incapable of waiting even a second longer.

When he had finished, he slumped in the doorway, wondering what F-69 would think of him now.

"Your turn to make me feel happy," she said, getting off her knees and tugging his arm.

He stared at her, comprehension dawning in his fogged brain. "My turn?" His cock stirred as tingles ran through his body.

F-69's sultry gaze didn't leave his while she slowly unbuttoned her blouse and took it off, then slid out of her skirt. Her underwear and bra seemed to be made of some sort of lacy, silken second skin, and he could see no straps, hooks or elastic bands. Her bra hugged her breasts like his hands longed to.

"Take it off," he said hoarsely.

She snapped her fingers, and the bra and panties slid to the floor. "Better?"

"Much." He could hardly breathe. He indicated the bed. "Lie down."

"As you wish." Her mouth curved in a grin and she licked her lips.

Steele waited until she had settled on the bed, then he pointed to her legs. "Wide open, please."

Her eyebrow lifted. "As my master commands. What else should I do?"

"Your master would like you to touch yourself."

He watched as she parted her silky, tight curls with her fingers, baring her sex. The tip of her index found her clit and she stroked it. She moaned softly and tilted her head back, baring her long, pale throat. Slick and pink, her labia seemed to beg him to kiss them and he didn't resist.

Climbing on the bed with her, he dipped his head between her legs and lapped at her pussy. Her sweet flesh swelled gently beneath his touch, and he found her clit and nibbled it with his lips. She uttered a cry and raised her hips, pressing his mouth harder to her slippery cunt. Tremors swept over her, and wetness flooded her pussy, exciting him with its heady taste. His cock stiffened even more.

"That feels so good," she gasped.

"You taste so good," Steele moaned, diving his tongue into her flesh, swirling it in circles around her hard clit. He slid one, then two fingers into her tight passage and gently fluttered them, eliciting a loud gasp and another hot flood of liquid from F-69.

Steele drew back a bit to get a glimpse of his fingers working into her cunt. He loved the way her flesh hugged him. Her short curls tickled his fingers and chin, and he lowered his head once more to nudge her clit with his tongue.

"Oh, yes, oh, yes," she sang.

"Tell me what you like," Steele ordered.

She stopped moving her hips and thought for a minute. "I like when you lick my clit, and your fingers moving inside me felt good." A little quiver ran through her and she said, "Don't stop now, please."

"Are you on birth control?" Steele raised himself on his forearms and looked down at her. "I don't want you to worry, so I have to tell you that—"

"I'm an android," she blurted, her face suddenly turning bright red.

Then he saw a tear in the corner of her eye. Realization struck him. Androids were half machine. Of course she couldn't get pregnant—they were made, not born.

"I'm sorry. Hey, why are you crying?"

"Just shut up and make love to me," she said in an uncharacteristic outburst of emotion.

She trembled in his arms, her body as tense as a violin

string. He had the impression he held a half-wild creature, and instinctively he pressed his lips to hers, soothing her with a kiss.

Her mouth opened to his, deepening the kiss, her tongue doing things to his that drove him wild. He reached down and guided his stiff cock into her passage.

As soon as her tight cunt clamped over his cock, she wrapped her long legs around his waist and drummed his buttocks with her heels. He thrust, letting the full length of his shaft slide into her.

"Harder!" she begged.

"I don't know if I can hold off much longer."

Damn the thawing out. He was so highly sensitized he couldn't control his cock one bit. It was about to blow its top off. His balls contracted nearly to his stomach and he couldn't stop quivering. His cockhead pounded against her womb, and a sudden hard pulsing rush through her cunt, sucking at him. A wave of pleasure submerged him. It felt like he was drowning in lust. He could hardly breathe.

"I can't stop it," he cried harshly.

"Don't stop! I'm coming," she screamed, grabbing him with her legs and arms, bucking beneath him.

He hung on, jets of seed shooting from his cock until he thought he would pass out. Rolling off her, he rested his head on her shoulder and closed his eyes.

"How do you feel?" she asked, stroking his cheek.

"Like a deflated balloon," he admitted. He cleared his throat. "Don't you have another name than F-69? I don't like calling you a serial number all the time."

"I'm just an android," she said.

Her voice sounded funny so he opened his eyes and propped himself on his elbow.

She smiled at him, but he saw the sadness in her eyes.

"What's so bad about being an android? I think you're terrific," he added.

"It's not bad, but you see, in a few months, or weeks, or even days I can be obsolete. When that happens, all the androids who don't have a permanent job and home are taken back and refurbished." She gave him a wobbly smile.

"What does refurbished mean?"

"It means they...scrap me and make a new and better model." Bravely she hung on to the remains of her cheerful grin.

A splinter of ice lodged in Steele's heart. "Take you away? They can't do that. I... I need you." He swallowed. He had never, ever said that to anyone and he'd always sworn never to get tied down. But this was different... F-69 was different, and he realized with a start that he truly did need her — perky voice, bright smile and all.

She leaned over and kissed him on the lips, her mouth brushing against his as lightly as a butterfly's wings. "We learn to live day by day, and not look too far into the future."

"I can't accept that. Besides, I've been propelled into the future whether I liked it or not."

Steele sat up and looked down at her. Her hair spread out on the pillow in a bright, fiery cloud and her eyes stared up at him, twin sapphires that sparkled with myriad emotions. How could they consider for a minute scrapping such a treasure?

"I think it's time I talked to someone." He got out of the bed and pulled on his clothes.

"What are you doing?" F-69 asked.

Steele grinned. "Take me to your leader."

Her eyebrows rose. "Are you sure?"

"It's time I took control of my life again. I wasn't made to lie in bed all day, no matter how agreeable," he added.

"All right." F-69 nodded. "Your quarantine is over now, anyway. I will make an appointment for you. This evening, you will watch the hologram tape about our government, and then tomorrow I will take you to my superior, who can talk to you about your future."

"Agreed." Steele was not looking forward to another educational hologram, but a second thought formed in his mind.

"Why are you smiling?" asked F-69.

"I'm thinking about tonight, and a big bubble bath for two."

One of the things he liked about his room was the bath. It had a giant Jacuzzi-style tub and a walk-in shower big enough for an elephant.

* * * *

Steele ran the bath. He slid into the tub and waited until F-69 joined him. Then he took some of her soap and rubbed it all over her body. She did the same to him, lingering on his long thighs and flat stomach, and over that fascinating part of his anatomy that changed shape and size whenever she touched it.

In fact, his whole body fascinated her. The hardness of his muscles and the dark, curly hair on his chest and legs astounded her. F-69 made him stand up so that she could see and touch him all over. His flat, hard chest was soon decorated with her soapy handprints. She loved making love to him. His cock grew hard when she touched it, yet his testicles remained soft. And when he grew hard, his body trembled a bit at her touch.

He had to sit down, after she'd pushed and pulled, tickled and touched his cock. His face was flushed and he seemed out of breath.

"Are you all right, Old Timer?" F-69 teased.

He grinned. "I am over six thousand years older than you, so I guess Old Timer is right. But I'll show you what this old guy can do."

"Show me what?"

"What we can do in a bathtub," said Steele, standing, and he rubbed soft soap over her body.

Now, both covered with fragrant lather, wherever their bodies touched, they slid. Sensations were different now. Hands and arms were slippery, and when Steele nudged her legs apart with his thigh, they opened as if buttered.

And when he plunged into her, she was soon gasping with pleasure under Steele's skillfully gentle thrusts.

He withdrew and turned her around. He parted her legs and touched her sopping wet pussy. "Do you want me?" he asked.

"Yes! Please," F-69 begged, bending over. He took her from behind, curling over her body, his chest pressed to her back. It was incredible. The fullness of his cock entering her, his hands clutching at her waist, the sexy words whispered in her ear — it was almost too much. Her whole body expanded to meet him, and when his cock plunged inside her, she never wanted it to end.

He drove his cock deeper inside her, each thrust nearly lifting her off her knees. One hand massaged her breasts, and the other hand reached under her belly to tickle her clitoris. F-69 braced herself on the edge of the tub and pushed backward, feeling the waves of pleasure clenching her stomach and thighs. But Steele stopped his hard thrusts and withdrew, teasing her, circling her labia with the tip of his shaft until she begged him to take her once more. Now that she knew what the outcome would be, her body shivered in anticipation.

"Please, take me," she begged.

"Oh, I will," he said, his voice thick.

He parted her buttocks, and slowly, ever so slowly, pushed his finger into her butt, all the while rubbing her clit skillfully with one finger, another finger deftly plunging into her throbbing pussy. F-69 gasped as her body's senses seemed to go into overdrive. She moved her hips up and down, grinding her sex harder into Steele's fingers. She wanted more.

For a while he teased her, stretching her gently, making her want to scream with frustration. She tried to gather her thoughts to tell him, but all she could feel was his agile fingers probing her body, touching her in places that both tickled and ached. An urgent pressure built in her belly that made her pant, that made her nipples so hard they hurt, and that made her want to feel something huge penetrate her body. She needed something bigger!

"More," she managed to gasp, rubbing her butt frantically against his belly. She caught his erection between her thighs and squeezed.

Steele uttered a moan and withdrew his finger. He put more slippery soap on her ass. Then the thick head of his penis pushed her tight muscles. The tickling rub of his penis as it slowly moved into her sensitive anus drove her wild. Steele moved slowly and gently, but it was all the more exciting for it. Inch by inch, she let him past her tight ring of muscle. As he eased into her body, he softly touched her clit. The sensations threatened to overwhelm her. Her body was at a fever pitch. She didn't know anymore where his body left off and where hers began.

Once he had half-sheathed his cock within her bottom, he gently moved it in and out, until F-69 suddenly bucked and started to shriek, her vagina and her buttocks pulsing in unison on his cock and on his fingers. Steele cried out too, holding her tightly to his chest as he ejaculated into her, his body thrusting and thrusting, his hips grinding into hers.

F-69 realized that he had shared her pleasure. She didn't worry that he would hurt himself anymore, even when he cried out. She was also glad that the chambers were soundproofed.

Steele got his breath back and looked at her. They were sitting in the tub, face to face now, arms and legs entwined.

"Tomorrow we'll go see my superior, and then you will be able to leave. You will have the chance to make your life somewhere else."

"How could I leave you now? Your lessons are going so well," he said, a note of teasing in his voice.

F-69's hands trembled and she clenched them. Her heart was breaking, but she was nothing if not realistic. "You have your whole life in front of you."

"No." His eyes were serious. "We have our whole lives in front of us."

Her head was swimming from fatigue and too much excitement. She tried to argue, but it ended up as a yawn. She sighed deeply and leaned her head on his broad chest. "We'll talk about it tomorrow," she said.

Afterward, he rinsed her off and carried her to her bed. F-69 was vaguely aware of his hands smoothing the covers over her body and she fell into a deep, dreamless sleep.

* * * *

The next day, Steele woke up early. He reached out his arm, but F-69 was gone. His bed was empty. He called her name and she appeared, a tray of food in her hands.

"Eat. The appointment is in half an hour."

"I didn't see the educational hologram yet," he teased.

F-69 smiled, but it was a small smile. "Just be ready soon."

He wanted to ask what was the matter, but his experience with women was limited. He had been married for a brief time, but his wife had walked out on him. She had claimed his work was more important than their relationship and looking back, he figured she was probably right. He dressed, and F-69 came in and led him to the doorway.

"Put your hand on this pad," she instructed, "and say your name aloud so that your identity will be carried throughout the station and you will be able to enter any doors."

He did, and there came a faint tingle as a light played up and down over his hand. Then the door in front of him slid up with a whisper. He found himself staring at a long corridor. On one side were doors, and the other side was made up of windows, overlooking the vastness of outer space. For a minute he stood still, getting used to the feeling of standing in the middle of a gigantic spaceship. It was one thing to know something, and another to actually see it.

"Are you all right? I can make the windows opaque if you like."

"No, I'm fine. It's…beautiful," he managed.

The hall curved gently around to the left, beige walls, white tiled floor, white doors... The color scheme was designed to soothe and yet interest the mind. Huge windows gave breathtaking views. There were even planters embedded in the walls. Strange ferns and ivy, and plants he could not identify trailed to the floor adding dashes of color.

"This is the living wing, where all the non-crew members of the spaceship have their quarters. The crew is on the other side of the ship. If we go to the right, we will arrive at the gym, and past that is the laboratory. Here is a map. There are maps on every floor and in the hallways. Look for this icon and you will..."

"Just take me to the person in charge of me," Steele said. "We can learn about maps and icons and the ship's layout another time. All right?"

"Sorry, I'm just a little...despondent," she said.

"Why?"

She stared at him, her expression resolutely cheerful despite her unhappy eyes. "Because you are going to ask for your independence and you will no longer need a nanny-teacher android."

"Is that what you are?" A smile quirked at the corner of his mouth.

"Yes." She turned suddenly and walked off to the left. "Follow me."

At the end of the hallway was an elevator. Its door slid up as they approached, and when Steele entered he remarked on several sets of commands. "They still use letters and numbers I recognize."

F-69 pushed the number 8 and said, "Yes, the Federation uses five official alphabets and numerical systems. And—"

"Tell me about the person we're going to see." He wanted to head off her lecture about the Federation. His brain would explode if he learned one thing more.

She pouted, obviously disappointed not to be giving a lecture. "You'll be seeing Executive Marchon. She is the liaison in charge of your dossier. Any decisions about you will go through her. The real decisions are taken far from here on Main Planet. Main Planet is the center for the Federation where—"

"And decisions are made quickly?" Steele interjected, not wanting to hear about the principal exports, demography and climate of Main Planet.

She sighed. "They are made instantly."

The elevator stopped and let them out at a new hallway, where the walls were dark blue and the floor had been done in beautiful dark, polished wood set in a chevron pattern. This hallway had the same huge windows and followed the same curve, so Steele supposed the station must be built along the lines of an ocean cruiser.

Curious, he went to the window and looked out. Dizziness swept over him as he stared into emptiness. Below, the space station dropped out of sight, like a huge city floating upside-down. It gave him vertigo. He glanced upward and saw the same thing in the other direction. Like a hundred skyscrapers melded together and floating in outer space. Nothing he'd ever seen compared to this, and as he watched, a small spaceship appeared then swung around to dock at a special area on the space station near the tip.

He pointed. "Is that a little space scooter?"

F-69 glanced up and shook her head. "No, that's a transport vessel. It looks small from here, but it's three hundred feet long."

Steele gulped. The station was gigantic.

"Come on, Executive Marchon is waiting for you." F-69 opened a door and stepped back, motioning him inside. "I will wait for you here."

The door whispered shut behind him.

F-69 watched as Steele disappeared inside the office, then she went to stand near the window. Her whole body ached. She was sore because of the sex—yes, there was that. But it was an agreeable soreness. Her heart was sore as well, but that was because Steele was going to leave soon. She had no doubt about that. He was smart, capable and had skills that would certainly interest the Federation. No, her body ached because she was stressed. It didn't take a *psy* to tell her that. Most androids her age had already been recycled. She had been retained because of Steele, her favorite student. Soon, though, she would get the call. And, for her, it would all be over.

Her forehead pressed against the glass, she stared into the vastness of space. Stars twinkled. A spaceship made its slow approach to the station, its landing lights flashing. In the distance, just visible above the top of the station, a huge carrier ship was just taking off, on its way to a faraway planet to bring supplies. Maybe she should stow away on one of the ships leaving the station. She could hide from the Federation, maybe get some fake papers, pretend to be human. If caught, she would be sentenced to death, though. Androids were forbidden from masquerading as humans.

She sighed. It would do no good. She was useless, except as a teacher. And no one was interested in hiring a pedantic robot who could only spout endless information about the blasted Federation.

Chapter Eleven

Steele entered the office. A stout, middle-aged woman sat at a huge desk, a stack of black disks in front of her. There was no clutter. The computer terminal had been reduced to voice commands, a folding keyboard, a floating screen and tiny disks that held as much information as a super-terminal had in his time. He had learned all that from his holo. Technology had become practically invisible, so Executive Marchon's desk was bare.

She motioned him to the chair in front of her desk. "How are you, Mr. Steele?"

"Fine, thank you."

"I hear from F-69 that you have acclimated and are ready to take your place in our society."

Steele nodded. "If there is such a place, yes."

She cocked an eyebrow. "Do you have any doubts?"

"I'd be a fool not to doubt."

"Tell me, Mr. Steele" She called up a floating screen and consulted it. "What were you doing when you landed in that frozen lake?"

The question came out of left field and startled him. "I-I was searching for two people. That was my job. I was a tracker."

"And did you find them?" She propped her chin on her hands and studied him intently.

Steele had to reflect for a minute. "I think so. I remember seeing the woman—she waved, and we set the helicopter down. After that, nothing." He frowned then shook his head.

"What is it?"

"You're not going to believe me."

"Try me." The eyebrow shot upward again.

"One of the people I was tracking supposedly came from another time. He had been trapped in the ice and had woken up after, hell, I don't know, a thousand years. The government hired me to find him for them. The man had gone missing along with a woman, and they needed him for some experiments. You wouldn't have anything in your files about him, would you?"

Executive Marchon smiled. "You're not going to believe me."

"Try me." He grinned.

"Here is an old holo. It's a copy of a copy of a copy of a... copy." She waved her hand. "Six thousand years is a long time."

A floating screen appeared and Steele's eyes widened. The picture was faint and trembled a bit, but there on the screen was the man he had been seeking. He sat on a snowmobile. Standing next to him was a short, stocky woman with a round face, a mass of coppery curls and bright, light-brown eyes. She held a small child in her arms, and all three wore Eskimo garb.

The man gazed out of the screen and said something. The red-haired woman translated. She said, "There are many people interested in how our ancestors lived. My husband, Kellorin, is busy most all of the year organizing special camping trips and giving talks, but he always takes time off to spend with his family."

Steele watched, fascinated, as the man from the past spoke of his life. There were film shots of him building an igloo, spearing fish in a river, and him making a bow and arrow set. The red-haired woman translated everything he said, and between them Steele could see the close bond that united them. Humor and love shone out of their eyes when they looked at each other, and with a pang he thought of F-69.

When the interview ended, a commercial came on telling

about a camping trip to the great north with the man as a guide.

"Did you find this informative?" Executive Marchon leaned forward over her desk.

"Incredible. A man from the past..." Steele winced. That described him.

"I showed that to you for several reasons. One reason is to show you that there is a place for you in this time, just as Kellorin found a place in your time. But the most important is this — thanks to that man, space travel became possible. Many things became possible, actually. It was a huge step forward for science. You found him, or, rather, because of you, Kellorin was found. He agreed to take part in several important experiments, and cryogenics was perfected."

Steele nodded, bemused. "So is there a campground reserved for me too?"

"Would it interest you if there was?"

"It's what I do best. Tracking lost tourists in the wilderness." He scratched his head. "Is there still wilderness on planet Earth?"

"Earth? That would be a waste of your talent. The only wilderness left there are tiny parks. No, I was thinking more along the lines of a forest planet, Amazonia. It's in a protected zone and has been declared a galactic park and treasure. There are hundreds of hotels and camping grounds there, all carefully ecologically controlled. But people will wander off the trails and get lost. If you agree, you'll be put in charge there. You'll be head ranger and have a couple thousand people working for you. It's not a park, it's a planet. You'll be in charge of it as the warden."

Steele shook his head, struck speechless. Finally, he managed to say, "A planet? I... It sounds perfect, thank you. But..."

"But?"

He hesitated then blurted, "I'm not sure how your protocol works for this, but I want to keep F-69 with me."

"Really? She's almost obsolete. We can get you a newer,

more efficient model, and besides, you won't be needing her academic lecturing all the time."

Steele grimaced. "I've grown accustomed to her lectures. Actually, I've gotten quite fond of her."

"Are you sure? Once you give her a permanent home, she will be bound to you. It's like marriage."

The thought had occurred to him. The word marriage, though... He hated that word. "But it's not exactly like marriage."

Executive Marchon shook her head. "No. Androids are forbidden to marry. They cannot have children and they cannot vote or hold positions in the government."

Shocked, Steele said, "You treat them like slaves."

"In a way, they are. They are built, not born, and they cannot reproduce. They are made for certain functions."

Steele looked at Executive Marchon. In a low voice he said, "My first wife left me after we tried to have kids and the fault turned out to be mine. I turned back to my work, and she simply left me. I never wanted to marry again. I made that mistake once. I'm sterile. I can't have children, and neither can F-69, so in a way we're perfect for each other." He held her gaze. "So if you send me away to this planet, send F-69 with me. Please."

She sighed. "I'll put in the request, but I can't guarantee anything. The decision is not mine to make. Besides, you might want to think of F-69's preferences. She is a city-bot, and has never to my knowledge been off this space station to go anywhere. At any rate, I'd ask her if I were you." Executive Marchon stood and shook his hand. "You may leave now. I'll get in touch with you as soon as everything is ready."

Steele left the office and joined F-69, who had been waiting for him in the hallway.

"How did it go? Can you tell me?" she asked.

"I have to think about it for a while." His chest tightened. Could he take her with him? Would she agree? He hoped so, but he was afraid to get his hopes dashed. "How about a tour of the station?" he asked her.

She opened her mouth as if to say something, then she shrugged. "Come. I bet you've never seen anything as amazing as this place."

She took him on a guided tour of the space station. It wasn't that amazing to him. Except for the mind-boggling views of outer space, the station was just like a combination high-class hotel and university. Instead of classrooms, there were stations where beings in various stages of cryonic sleep were tended to by groups of scientists.

After seeing twenty or more such stations, Steele turned to F-69. "This is very interesting."

She beamed.

"But is there a place we can go to..." He struggled to put words to his thoughts. "A park or something?"

"A park?" She nibbled her lower lip. "I noticed how you paused almost every time we passed a window," she said. "Our records show you were used to living outdoors, so this must be hard for you."

"I don't like being closed in," he admitted. "What about you, F-69? What do you think of the wilderness?"

"I grew up in a space station and the city. I don't know anything about the wilderness."

Steele felt a prickle of disquiet. "Would you like to learn more?"

She didn't answer at first, further worrying him, then she said, "I know a place we can go that you might like. Follow me." She led him to another elevator and pressed her hand on the palm lock. Then she pushed the bottom button.

"The basement? Is that where your greenhouse is?"

Her eyes twinkled. "Not exactly."

They stepped out into an all-black hallway. It had no windows and led for what seemed a long time in a straight line. Then Steele noticed something.

"We're going downhill."

"It's very subtle. I'm surprised you noticed." She motioned

to a black steel door set in the black wall. "After you."

He opened the door and stepped into space.

For a moment his body tensed and he grabbed instinctively at the doorway, but he wasn't falling. He stood on a platform, and all around him was glass, and all around them space stretched to infinity.

"The space station is above us now," said F-69. "But don't look up. It will ruin the effect. This is an observation deck, a view port and a meditation center. Come. Let me show you." She walked out, and since the platform had been made of glass, it was as if she floated in space.

Steele let out his breath. He had never been stunned by beauty before, but this amazed him. Space was not empty. It glittered with diamond frostings of stars. Green, red and blue nebulae hung like fireworks frozen in time, along with swaths of softly scintillating clouds.

Planets orbited nearby. One had five moons, and one was so close it took up nearly a fifth of the view.

"We are in orbit around that planet," said F-69, pointing at the reddish giant. "The darker marks you see on the surface are cities. On the other side of the planet there is an ocean. As it revolves we will see it. Come, lie down here. This is called a Zen-couch."

Steele, dumbfounded by the view, lay on a reclining couch made of soft, warm, transparent material. The couch seemed to adjust to his body, cuddling him in a relaxing embrace. He patted the couch. "Come closer to me," he said.

She lay next to him, her head on his shoulder. "Did Executive Marchon say anything about when you would be leaving?"

He couldn't tell what she was thinking from her voice. She was back in her 'nanny-teacher' mode.

"She said she'd contact me."

"Oh."

"F-69, can I...? Do you have...? I mean, it's your name. Isn't there anything else I can call you?"

Instead of answering, she pointed to a faint white smudge in the distance. In the vastness of space, it was hard to tell how far it was but it seemed very far away. "There is the Milky Way galaxy. Where you're from."

He caught her slender wrist in his hand. "Fiona."

"What is that?"

"A name. Your name is Fiona."

In the soft light cast from the stars he saw shock on her face. "You can't give me a name. It's not right."

"I can give you my name. Steele. Your name will be Fiona Steele when we're married."

To his dismay her face twisted and tears spilled from her eyes. "Stop it," she whispered. "You can't. It's not allowed."

"I don't know if it's the view, or if it's the couch, but I feel as if I can do anything, even fly from here to the Milky Way galaxy in a heartbeat. This place is magic." He pulled her to him and kissed her full lips. "It's magic, and I love you."

"I love you too." She sobbed even louder. "But I can't marry you."

"Is it me? Knowing that I can't live in a city or place like this?" Steele asked. He feared her answer. Maybe she hated the idea of living in the wilderness.

But her answer was even worse than he imagined. "I'm obsolete. In two days, I'm going to be refurbished, recycled and my memory banks will be scrapped."

"What?" Steele cradled her in his arms and swore. "No, I won't let that happen."

"You can't do much about it, I'm afraid." She grew still and took a deep breath. "We just have to enjoy the time we have left."

"Stop it. I told you I won't let that happen."

"Besides, I can never have children. It's not fair for a human to marry an android." Her eyes were still filled with tears.

"I can't have children, either. See? We're more alike than you think." Steele kissed her softly on the lips, his tongue tracing their contours before dipping between them and touching the tip of her sweet tongue. "Can we go back to the room?"

Slipping her hand into his pants, she fondled his cock. "Making love on a Zen-couch is something everyone has to try."

"Right here? But anyone can come in and find us." He thought his blood had suddenly caught on fire. The couch vibrated subtly.

"It matters not. Take off your clothes," said Fiona, unbuttoning his shirt.

He did, and lay on the couch. What material made up the Zen-couch? As soft as satin, elastic, yet firm. It seemed almost alive. And when his naked skin touched it, a thrill ran through his body. A small part of his brain wondered if anyone would open the door and come in. What if they were seen? Incredibly, the thought made his cock stiffen even more.

Fiona stripped off her dress and slid onto the couch next to him. The stars, the planets, the impression of being nude in the infinity of space, made his head spin. His cock hardened as Fiona stroked it, her hand gliding slowly across his sensitive skin.

"Don't move," she said. "Lie here and let me give you pleasure. Watch the dance of the stars and the planets. Feel the song of space in your bones." Her mouth bruised his in a hard kiss, then she pulled back and raked her fingernails lightly over his chest, down to the wiry hair on his groin.

She fastened her mouth around his cock and a tight heat surrounded it. A wave of desire shot through him and he lifted his hips, thrusting his cock farther into her mouth. Then her finger found his anus and tickled him, and an electric shock zinged from her touch to the tip of his head.

His mouth suddenly dry, he focused his eyes on the slowly revolving planet as his body went into overdrive. He didn't want to move, but how to control the urge to thrust his hips upward?

To resist or not to resist? Not to resist. He reached down and took Fiona's shoulders in his hands and pulled her up so that she straddled his lap, her knees on either side of his hips.

"Sit," he ordered.

She looked so lovely, with her long red hair tousled around her shoulders. "Yes, master," she purred.

She sat, and when her sex touched the tip of his cock she hesitated then pushed herself down, impaling her body on his. Her cunt slid over his cock as if he had been greased. Holding his breath, he stared at her, thinking that he had never seen such a beautiful woman in his life. Such a beautiful, sexy woman. She grinned then twisted her hips. The friction as her cunt rubbed up and down his cock made him gasp.

"Shall I stop?"

"No!" Grabbing her thighs, he raised his hips so that her knees barely reached the couch and her full weight rested on him. The tip of his cock touched her womb as he thrust.

She uttered a low cry and leaned forward, and her nipples brushed across his chest. He wanted to cup her soft breasts in his hands. He was going to take them in his mouth and suck her nipples. Those thoughts made his cock even stiffer, and a rush of cum surged from him. His balls tightened and he braced his legs against the couch, thrusting faster and faster until Fiona's body started to convulse. The tip of his cock tingled, then he came, pouring himself into her, holding tightly to her waist and shoulders, wrapping his legs around her, and below them the majesty of space took away what was left of his breath.

Then he heard the sound of the door opening.

Steele leaped off the Zen-couch, snatched the first thing he saw and flung it on his waist. It was Fiona's dress. She raised herself on her elbows and smiled at him.

"We have no taboos about sex or nudity. But a big strong man in a skimpy yellow skirt might raise a few eyebrows."

She handed him his pants. "If it makes you feel better, take these. They suit your coloring better."

* * * *

The contract arrived the next day in his mail. A real letter, written on fine paper that when he unfolded it lost all signs of the fold. For a minute he didn't even read the letter, he was too busy trying to figure out what kind of paper it was. Then two words caught his attention.

'Amazonia' and 'F-69'.

He read, his heart pounding.

Mr. Steele,

Your job will start immediately. Please go to flight deck fifteen at seven p.m. and board the Kingly Liner bound for Amazonia. Your request to keep F-69 with you has been accepted. She will accompany you to Amazonia. Her ownership papers will be sent to you.

Best wishes,

Executive Marchon

Steele carefully tucked the paper in his pocket and looked at the woman standing at his side.

"It says you can come with me," he said.

A wash of red infused her cheeks. "I was afraid to ask," she said. Then she grinned. "You're going to love Amazonia, and I can't wait to start telling you all about it. Did you know that at the equator — ?"

He put his hand over her lips. "Fiona Steele, I am only going to say this once," he said sternly.

"Be quiet?" she said, her lips brushing the palm of his hand.

"No, I love you," he said, and he kissed her. "Actually, I believe I will say that once a day, or once an hour." He laughed at the look of relief in her blue eyes. "And you know what else?"

"What?" she asked.

"I am looking forward to my new life," he said. "With you."

"And you know what I think?"

"What?"

"We have to celebrate." She pushed the button on the wall.

"Hel-lo. I. Am. The. Re-fri-gor-a-tor. What. Do. You. Want?"

Fiona leaned toward the wall. "A bowl of strawberries, whipped cream and melted chocolate."

Steele's eyebrows rose.

They rose even farther when Fiona took the tray with the food and said, "Into the bedroom, Steele."

In the bedroom, she stripped off her dress, lay back on the bed and drizzled chocolate over her belly. She dipped her finger in the whipped cream, put some on her breasts, and topped each one with a strawberry. "I'm waiting," she said.

Steele took off his clothes and climbed onto the bed.

He lowered his head and took one of her nipples in his mouth, first eating the strawberry and licking the whipped cream. His cock hardened instantly and Steele groaned. This would be some test for his capabilities.

Fiona lay back and took a strawberry from the bowl and ate it slowly. Then she pointed to her other breast. "Over there," she said.

His member grew so hard it ached. He wanted to thrust it right away into Fiona's hot cunt to ease his need, but he moved slowly, savoring each instant. He parted Fiona's legs and after a last nibble on her whipped-cream-covered nipple, he traced a trail of kisses from her breasts down to the pool of melted chocolate on her belly, to her parted thighs. He stopped there, getting a firm hold on himself, and kissed her inner thigh. Her flesh was as smooth as the finest satin. His tongue followed the curve of her thigh to the hollow near her hip, then he slid down to her pussy.

She gave a mewl of impatience and thrust her hips upward.

"Stop!" he ordered, giving her a strong shake. "If you move or speak, I will stop. Do you want that?"

"No," she whispered. Her eyes widened and she stopped writhing.

"If you don't obey, I will spank you," he said, his voice stern.

Fiona stiffened. "Yes, master," she whispered.

A pang of sheer excitement shook Steele. "Do you want me to spank you?" he asked a little breathlessly. Did she hate being spanked? Or would she let him do it?

"If I'm naughty, you can spank me." Fiona sighed. "You can put me over your knees and spank me. And if you want, sometimes I'll be bad just to get a spanking." She looked coquettishly at Steele from beneath lowered eyelashes. "Would you ever give me a spanking?" she murmured.

"I'll do just that," said Steele. He shivered. The thought of bending her over his knees and slapping her smooth buttocks was making his cock twitch.

"Oh, yes, please do," she whispered, arching her back a bit.

With a groan, he sat up then pulled her over onto his lap. Her buttocks rose like two hills and he lifted his hand and brought it down with a soft slap.

"Harder," she said.

He obliged, and she writhed.

"Harder!" she shouted.

He spanked and spanked, until her buttocks turned pink, and he was just about to explode — his cock pressed into her soft stomach.

"Take me now," she pleaded, rolling off his lap and spreading her legs.

Her body gave off a heady scent and her cunt looked slick and swollen with desire.

He put his mouth to her pussy, greedily sucking and licking. She bucked and he held her still while his tongue flicked over her clit. She writhed harder now, little cries coming from her throat.

"Again! More! Faster!" she gasped.

"Quiet!" he begged, holding her still.

She tried not to move, but he could tell his teasing set her on fire. It amused him to be in control of her splendid body. He held her still, leaning on her with his forearms so she couldn't move. Dipping his fingers into her cunt, he watched as her flesh swelled and reddened. He used his tongue to tickle her clit, and her breathing grew labored as she tried not to wiggle. But her heart was pounding madly and little tremors ran through her arms and legs.

He drove his tongue into her cunt, delighting in her taste and perfume. She was so wet his face was soon covered with her juices, and he knew that in a moment he would explode. He wanted to keep on teasing her, but aching pressure was building in his loins. Soon he would be unable to control himself. His cock throbbed in time to his pounding heart and his head started to feel as if it would fly off his shoulders. Steele rose onto his elbows and guided his cock into Fiona's hot pussy.

She came at once, crying his name so loudly and startling him so much he thought he would have a heart attack. When she finished, he let go, ejaculating into her body with all the force built up since that morning. All the energy he had managed to accumulate holding himself together made his orgasm explosive. He had to grab on to Fiona to keep from flying to pieces. For the first time ever, making love nearly made him weep. He shuddered into her, his seed spurting out, and each spurt jolted like an electric current. Finally, his body stopped convulsing and he managed to raise his head.

"Strawberries, whipped cream and a spanking. My very own planet. And an android to love. What more can I ask for?"

"Chocolate?" Fiona asked, batting her eyelashes.

Chapter Twelve

The Planet Amazonia stretched out before them, miles and miles of forest, jungle, tundra, field, and ocean. Several resorts had been built in different scenic places to cater to the most demanding luxury camper wannabe. As an ecological treasure, the planet was severely restricted to humans. Tourists were welcome, but only in certain areas. The impact of civilization was to be as minor as possible.

Of course, tourists being tourists, there were always one or two who wandered off the clearly indicated trails and invariably got lost. That was a problem, and to solve it, the Federation had hired a professional tracker — Steele.

Steele and Fiona had been unprepared for what awaited them. They were lodged in luxury apartments — in every single resort on the planet. Each resort had its tracking office, and Steele was in charge of them all. They couldn't get over it. Their own hover-copter. Their own apartments. Their own everything!

"No one on the space station owned anything," Fiona said to Steele. "We were all just part of the machine. Our rooms were temporary. We could be moved at any time. But this — this is our home, right? My balcony, my closet, my refrigerator, my cupboard, my towels." She took a towel from the shelf. "And....my bed." She sat on the wide expanse of satin sheet and stared up at Steele. "Do you know that — ?"

"Hush." Steele put his finger to her lips. "I have a feeling you're going to lecture me again about political or historical facts or about closets and towels, and I don't want to listen."

"You don't?" Hurt sparkled in her eyes. She pressed her

towel to her face, hiding her tears.

"No, I want to kiss you." He loved the way her expression cleared, the way her smile made her whole face glow.

Steele took the towel from her and gently wiped her face, pausing now and then to kiss her. Fiona giggled and pushed him away, but he persisted. She turned her back to him and he ran his hands down her spine, rubbing his thumbs into her muscles, kneading her back and ending up with his hands encircling her shoulders. Then he started to massage her neck, tickling her cheeks, and leaning down to nibble on her earlobe and lips.

She ended up kissing him back. Steele put his arms around her and pulled her down on the bed. When she was near him, touching him, her mouth on his, her hands roaming over his body, he simply couldn't imagine life without his adorable android.

Her eyes, that reflected each and every one of her thoughts, enchanted him. Her body was an electric charge. The scent of her skin was intoxicating. Steele was completely addicted to her.

He fastened his mouth on her slender neck and gave her a gentle love bite. He growled and bit her shoulder. Their lovemaking degenerated into a wrestling match. He was a pro—he had been on his college wrestling team. Fiona wasn't bad either.

Steele paused and drew a shaky breath. Legs sliding against legs, backs arching, bellies and hips touching. In a moment he would dissolve into a boneless shiver of desire.

Fiona gave a soft moan and twisted around, straddling his stomach. She leaned forward and kissed him, then he rolled over and pinned her beneath him. His cock pushed against her inner thigh, but she wasn't giving in yet. She wriggled away. He put his arms around her and tried to draw her to him. She just gave a deep chuckle and slid from beneath him with a movement like silk. She gasped and cried out in delight as he pulled her to him from behind. He thrust once, sheathing himself into her wet pussy.

Apparently however, Fiona decided he hadn't won quite yet. She scissored her legs and grabbed him around the torso. Using her body as a lever, she managed to throw him down. He was a bit hampered by his erection, but he easily avoided being pinned and slipped away again, his eyes dancing.

Steele was starting to get frustrated. Every time he thought he had her in a position to take her, she'd slip away. He would get the tip of his cock inside her, then she'd be gone. She was quick and lithe, and played dirty. Once, she even grabbed his balls. *That's cheating, isn't it?* If only it didn't *feel so good!* He could tell she was ready for him. Her nipples were taut, her pupils dilated, her pussy was soaking wet.

He tried every move in the book, but she knew more moves, and was far more flexible then he was. The wrestling match was too even, and he decided the best way to finish this game would be to surrender. He did so by grabbing Fiona around the neck and dragging her down on top of him. She arched her back and met him halfway. There was the shock of two bodies meeting. She opened her legs, urging him inside her, and urging him on. He thrust hard but slowed down, trying to keep himself from coming too fast — trying, and nearly succeeding.

But Fiona gave a soft cry and her body shuddered against his. That undid him. His movements accelerated, and his breath came in short gasps. Fiona rolled over and pushed him onto his back. Now she was on top, holding his shoulders, grinding her hips into his until he gave a hoarse cry and spent himself inside her. He shook from his head to the tip of his toes.

In the end, Steele wasn't sure who had won the wrestling match. He woke up on the floor. Fiona's and his body seemed to be twined together, along with all the satin sheets and covers on the bed that they had dragged down on top of them. He had fallen soundly asleep, as he usually did after a bout of lovemaking.

He wondered what had woken him then heard a small

cough. It was the resort's intercom system. He glanced up and saw that there was a screen in the corner of the room. He hoped it wasn't a two-way screen. The person's face in the screen looked worried.

"Yes," said Steele, blearily staring at the screen. "What is it?"

"Mr. Steele, I realize you just arrived, but there's an emergency. A tourist group has disappeared in the jungle. We need you to...er, to get dressed and go search for them."

So much for it not being a two-way screen.

"Will you be all right?" asked Fiona, sitting up and drawing the covers over her body. She glared at the screen. "Mr. Steele will be right with you. You can go away now." The face disappeared.

"I'll get them home by dinner," said Steele. He kissed his adorable android. *Life*, he thought, *cannot get much better*. He stood and leaned against the wall to get his balance.

A voice came from the wall. "I. Am. The. Re-fri-gor-a-tor. Would. You. Like. A. Cold. Beer?"

Things, he reflected, *could always get better*.

More books from
Totally Bound Publishing

Book one in the Heat series

For Murdoch, women are bad news. Trying to stay alive in war-torn Andalusia, tracking a vanishing femme fatal, hunted by The Brotherhood, the last thing he needs is love…

Alana expected salvation to come at a steep price, she just didn't think it would involve a collar.

Book one in the Out of Time series

*Moments before her death, medieval history student Lilly
Marten mysteriously arrives in the year 1503, where
soldier Gabriel Sutherland has been expecting her arrival.*

Thousands win homes off-planet. Too-good-to-be-true
questions turn deadly. It'll take more than wedding vows
to learn if happily-ever-afters are real.

About the Author

Samantha Winston

Samantha Winston is the pen name for sci-fi writer Jennifer Macaire. She lives in France with her husband, children, and two dogs. She grew up in upstate New York, Samoa, and the Virgin Islands. She graduated and moved to NYC where she modelled for five years for Elite. She went to France and met her husband at the polo club. All that is true. But she mostly likes to make up stories.

Samantha Winston loves to hear from readers. You can find contact information, website details and an author profile page at https://www.totallybound.com/

Home of Erotic Romance